I0755629

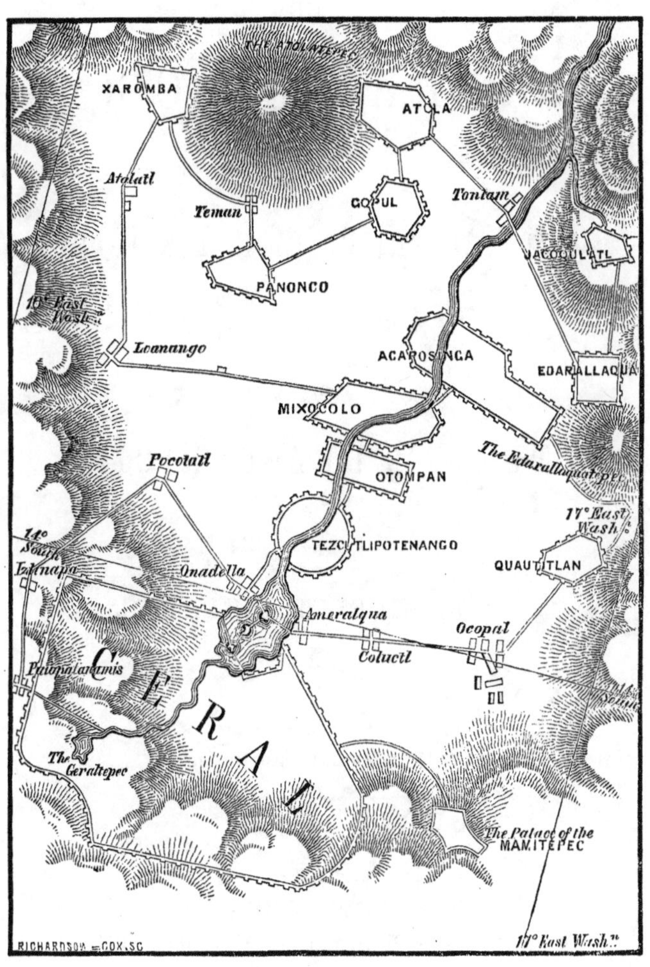
XAROMBA
ATOLA
Atolatl
Teman
COPUL
Tontam
PANONCO
Loanango
ACAPOSINGA
EDARALLAQUA
MIXOCOLO
The Edarallaquatepec
Pocotatl
OTOMPAN
17° East Wash.n
TEZCATLIPOTENANGO
QUAUTITLAN
Onadella
Ameralqua
Ocopal
Coluctl
CERAL
The Geraltepec
The Palace of the MAMITEPEC
RICHARDSON & COX.SC
17° East Wash.n

THE GERAL-MILCO;

OR

The Narrative of a Residence

IN A BRAZILIAN VALLEY

OF

THE SIERRA-PARICIS.

BY

A. R. MIDDLETOUN PAYNE.

With Map and Illustrations.

NEW YORK:
CHARLES B. NORTON, 71 CHAMBERS STREET,
IRVING HOUSE.
1852.

KITE & WALTON, PRINTERS.

TO

JOHN L. STEPHENS, Esq.,

This little volume

Is

Most respectfully dedicated,

As a slight expression of the esteem and

Admiration of one

Who would be his emulator in

Antiquarian Researches.

The Author.

INTRODUCTION

TO

PART FIRST.

Kind Reader :—

In thus presenting himself to your notice, for the first time, the author begs leave to state,—merely for his own interest,—that the substance of the following pages was not originally written with the intention of being published, but was comprised in a journal, kept for the amusement of his family and a few very intimate friends. But during a visit, recently made to the city of New York, several works, of a similar character to that which is now given up for inspection, were placed in his hands, and, on reading them, it appeared to him that the latter part of his travelling journal might, with but little trouble, be altered into a book, which, in its singularity, might equal, and, possibly, in its truth, excel, those with which he had met. Persuaded of this, he consulted the few who had read his narrative, and, fortified by their unanimous advice to have it exposed to the censorship of the public, he commenced his pleasant task of reducing it from its voluminous dimensions, to the size in which it now makes its appearance.

As to the *truth* of the work presented to you, the author will vouch for every word, although he has not sufficient vanity to let you read it without stating that he does not pretend to be anything like a good writer; and that his production is not given as an artistic performance, but as a plain and concise statement of facts,—of things that if disbelieved *now*, will soon be verified by future travellers. Bruce's great discoveries in Abyssinia were laughed at and scorned, by even the learned of the world, as the romantic effusions of a traveller who wished to ascertain how much the stay-at-homes could be fooled into crediting. *This* simple narrative merely tests and confirms the truth of the traditions current among the Quichuas of Peru, and may also be ridiculed and derided;—not that the author compares himself to James Bruce, for the orbit of the last is entirely beyond the reach of the former's vision, though not of his ambition.

The *discovery*,—if he may so term it,—that is narrated in the following pages will at least afford a solid foundation for men,—more learned than himself,—to erect an imperishable edifice upon.

The author finds it exceedingly difficult to inform the reader in what style the present composition is written, it being partly in the form of a narrative, and partly taken, *verbatim*, from the journal; but if this curious compound fails to give satisfaction, he believes that, at least, it is "something new."

Now, *considerate peruser*, your most humble servitor must confess that he has a particular dislike of those works, which are what is usually termed "spun out," and, in consequence, he has done his best not to be prolix. In carrying out this purpose it is not at all improbable but that he has fallen over the other side of the fence, and been entirely too concise. However that may be, whether his book is good, bad or indifferent, he presents it to you, leaving it to your better judgment to decide, requesting permission, at the same time, to sign himself, in advance,

Gentle reader, your most obliged and obedient servant,

A. R. MIDDLETOUN PAYNE.

Philadelphia, August 29th, 1849.

CONTENTS.

PART FIRST.

CHAPTER I.

CHAPTER II.

CHAPTER III.

CHAPTER IV.

CHAPTER V.

CHAPTER VI.

PART FIRST.

CHAPTER I.

The Start.

On Monday, August 16th 1847 I left the Charleston Hotel in Meeting Street, in company with Edward Laury Grey Esq,—who was to be my companion throughout my travels,—for the large brig Augusta, of Baltimore, bound for Rio Janeiro but which was to drop us at Para.

I had not yet seen the accommodations of the vessel as my friend Grey had arranged all the preliminaries without troubling me, for which I was very thankful,—and full of confidence in his talents for getting ready the 'fixings' necessary for such a voyage, I ascended the side, and stepped or rather stumbled on board; for the fact of the taffrail's being considerably above the level of the deck, entirely escaping my memory, I placed one foot on the top of the former and bringing my other one up too quickly, I lost my balance, and thinking it preferable to fall on a barrel of pickled pork than into the Cooper River, made a plunge forward, and the next second was sprawling on the top of the selected pedestal. However I soon 'righted myself' as the sailors would say, and getting into a more dignified position, looked around me.

Confusion worse confounded! The brig was taking in the fag end of the provisions for the voyage, and the men were rolling barrel on barrel of salt beef, pork, butter, and various other unpalatable edibles, so close to the extremities of our patent leathers, that Grey and I determined to evacuate this provisional department, and descended into the lower regions, that I might inspect the lodgings,—I positively have not, now, the assurance to call them 'accommodations,'—which had been *prepared* for us.

My stateroom was the first visited.

We both got in, somehow; and it is but fair that I should tell of the *state* in which it was. The two berths were without mattresses, pillows, sheets, or coverlid, being nothing but the slats on which all the above enumerated comforts are usually placed; two chairs in a very dilapidated plight comprised the sitting down conveniences. One of these was frightfully near being seatless, but this I subsequently remedied by tacking a stout India silk handkerchief over the frame,—while the other which was tetertortering on two legs, fortunately diagonally opposite each other, I rendered available by supporting one of the vacated corners on the ledge of the lower berth, and propping up the other by an apparatus consisting of the wall, a carpet bag, and a portable fishing rod; when thus arranged it could be used, but when seated upon it, the occupant had to be on the look out, for at best it was but a precarious situation.

The washstand was a fixture in the shape of a quarter segment of a circle, fastened in the corner behind the door, considerably interfering with the opening propensities of the latter, and forcing the person seeking an entrance, to slide in sideways, much to the danger of coat-tails from a preposterously large catch, set into the door-post.

Ned's stateroom was far better furnished than mine, but was much less clean, so leaving him to put to rights his vast chamber, I started on a tour of inspection in the centre cabin, or "saloon," to call it by the name with which it was complimented by the master of the brig.

Having come out of a stateroom, it had really an *imposing* appearance, and looked to me like quite a sizeable apartment, but in fact it was the smallest one I had ever seen, in a vessel of the Augusta's dimensions. Along the middle of it was a stationary mahogany dining, breakfasting and *suppering* table, all in one, which was amazingly far from clean. All around this fixture were backless benches, also cleeted to the deck and at a most uncomfortable distance from the eating board, so arranged, perchance, in accordance with a "notion" that, if a sudden lurch should occur while the passengers were at meals, the contents of their plates, and the condiments waiting to go on them, could slip on the floor between the edge of the table and the knees of the eaters. If this had been the intention, although it might have answered in common cases, on an uncommon one it did not, as I discovered, to the severe detriment of a new pair of inexpressibles.

Over the centre of the table depended a trio of swinging lamps, which being of a construction unsuited for ships, and burning oil of the odoriferous kind, had a very singular fancy, when filled and lit at supper, of sprinkling everything on the table that was within the range of their devastating showers.

On each side of the 'saloon,' were several doors leading into the staterooms, and at the end, a pair of folding doors admitted me to the private or ladies' cabin, which, for a wonder, was scrupulously clean and neat, forming, as may be imagined rather a strong contrast with what I had previously seen.

Having fully explored the premises I returned to Grey, and together we ascended the companion way to take a last glimpse at Charleston. As we stepped on deck, a tug—which had been getting up steam ever since we had come on board—let go her ropes, and the Augusta, being fastened to her, in five minutes we had started fairly on our long tour.

CHAPTER II.

The Voyage.—Arrival at Para.—Cause of the Expedition.—A Meeting on the Banks of the Dead Sea.—Object of the Expedition.

If I wished I could make a volume of our voyage alone, but as others have written on that subject numberless times, far better than I ever hope to, and as I do not wish to be long from the object of our tour and this book, I will give but a short account of my uncomfortablenesses. On the first night out I obtained a hammock, and had it swung in the ladies' cabin, which was unoccupied, where I slept very pleasantly every succeeding night, until our arrival at Havana on the Sunday morning following our departure. At this beautiful and musical capital, the Augusta remained until high tide on Tuesday morning, when, having received two feminine passengers among the several that came on board, I was obliged to retire to my proper stateroom when we sailed. In order to occupy my berth, my camp bedding had to be rummaged up from among the numerous bales of goods and packing cases directed to "Messrs. Payne and Grey, Para." However, it was found without much difficulty, and on Tuesday night I took up my quarters in the upper-berth, among the cockroaches, who expressed their disapprobation of my invasion of their territories by running over my hands and face in the most obstreperous manner. I got to sleep at last and slept pretty well until about two o'clock in the morning, when an unexpected and very severe sea struck the brig, tossing me from my elevated position to the floor, where I remained a few moments, covered with three carpet bags, the bedding, chairs, clothes, &c., &c. I got up, as soon as I could extricate myself, a good deal bruised, and fully recognizing the truth, "He that exalteth himself, shall be abased." I made up my bed in the lower berth and slept there every succeeding night that I was on board.

Now Grey and I are two of those fortunate few who never suffer from sea-sickness, and it was owing to this circumstance that we became acquainted with each other, which occurred in 1834, on board of an English ship on a voyage from Great Britain to St. Petersburg, on which occasion every soul, save us two, was down with it. Ned seeing that I was the only person in the cabin well enough to talk, introduced himself, and we commenced conversing. Since then we never went on any travels without being together. But if we were exempted, the servants which accompanied us on the present occasion, were not, all three of them being incapacitated from talking or walking.

The brig anchored off 'the flourishing town of Para,'—as the geographies have it,—on the morning of Wednesday, September the 15th, after a moderately quick passage of twenty-two days from Cuba. The sailors immediately commenced landing our merchandize and baggage.

The moon shone brightly over the wide harbor, silvering its placid waters as Ned and I bade adieu to some of our fellow-passengers, who had come on shore, immediately on the arrival of the Augusta, in the morning, to spend a day 'in town.' They were rowed off in one of the boats that had brought the last of our effects, and in a few moments after they got on board, the anchor was weighed, and the 'Brig Augusta, of Baltimore,' set sail for Rio Janeiro.

It is now time that the object of our expedition should be made known, and to do this it is necessary to learn, first, the cause, for which I must go back to the winter of 1845–6, when in company with Mr. Grey, I was travelling in Syria.

It was early in the evening of the first Saturday in the February of the latter year, that we pitched our tents on the shores of Lake Asphaltites, the once Vale of Siddim.

We had hardly done so, when one of the natives, attached to our little party, came to my tent and said that another American gentleman was at an encampment half a league further south. On hearing this both Grey and I remounted our horses, regardless of the fatigue we had endured from a long day's journey, and galloped to the designated spot. Here we found an *American*, certainly, but he was a native of Lima, and we were obliged to speak Spanish, instead of English, as we had hoped to be able to do. Nevertheless, we spent a very pleasant evening, and, during it, the conversation naturally turned upon travellers, thence to antiquarian researches, and, from this, to lost nations. Grey spoke of the ancient Peruvians and Mexicans, of their descendants' degeneracy, in having lost the arts and sciences of their ancestors, and of the generally received opinion that these two monarchies were ignorant of one another's existence. "It is true," here said the gentleman of Lima, "that such is the common opinion, but it is a mistaken one. The two nations of which you spoke, sir, not only know the situation, resources, civilization and government of each other's territory, but actually exchanged visits, if I may believe a hieroglyphical manuscript which I found, accidentally, among the wrecks of the once magnificent library of the Museum, in the city of Mexico. What I have already said, perhaps, astonishes you, but there is more to be told, which I learnt from the same manuscript. When Cortes, for the second time, entered the valley of Tenochtitlan, many of the inhabitants, contrary to the express commands of Guatemotzin, fled from their homes, and, penetrating through the territories of the Guatemalan kingdoms, entered,—after much fatigue, and much reduced in number,—the government of the Incas, taking up their residence in Cuzco. So far goes the scroll, but I can tell still more from traditions current among the Quichuas. The expatriated Mexicans had scarcely settled themselves in the above named city, when Pizarro and his followers, having murdered Atahuallpa, and Toparca having died, entered the capital, naming Manca as Inca. Notwithstanding their submission to the invaders, *all* the Peruvians were not satisfied with this rapid change of rulers, and many of them, together with the Mexicans, broke into the palace of the lately murdered Inca, (Atahuallpa) where his wives and children were still wailing at his death. The patriots and their friends persuaded several of these disconsolate beings to accompany them, and this little party set out to found an Incalate in the,—to them,—wilderness of Brazil.

"Five years since," continued the narrator, "I was spending a few weeks in the town of Villa Bella, near the source of the Rio Guapore, and on one occasion, being exceedingly fond of excursions and rambling walks, I accompanied a few friends to the foot of the Sierra Paricis, to stay two or three days there. On the second day we all set off, scrambling up the mountains. Most of the party gave out half way up, and when I got near the top, I found that I was alone. However, I persevered and reached the summit. Before me was spread the valley of the Incas! As I commenced descending towards the thickly built cities below me, my progress was arrested by several men, wearing the dress ascribed to the ancient Peruvians,—who sprung out of a covert, and obliged me to retrace my steps, telling me in the Aucaquis language, which I fortunately understood, that no armed stranger, which I unhappily chanced to be,—was admitted into their valley, which they call Geral.* The following day our party returned to Villa Bella,

* The reader will notice that on some maps the Sierra is named the *Geral Mountains*. It is, therefore, probable that the author and his friend were not the first to penetrate this singular territory.

and you, gentlemen, are the first persons who have ever heard of my adventure, and its vexatious termnation."

This speech was the cause of our expedition, and the object of it was to gain an entrance into this unvisited, and nearly unknown, valley. To effect this we had decided upon assuming the character of merchants, and in this, the most peaceful guise we knew of, we started for the Geral-milco.*

* This being the first time that the title of our volume is introduced, we take the opportunity of explaining that '*Milco*' is an Aztecan word signifying Valley.

CHAPTER III.

Departure from Para.—Character of Baggage.—The Rio Tapajos.—A Meeting in the Wilderness.

WE remained at Para until Saturday morning, September 18th, when we embarked on board of a small schooner, called the 'St. Joao,' bound for the town of Santarem, at the confluence of the Tapajos and Amazon, where we intended to procure a boat of some kind or other, to take us up the former river as far as we wanted to go, which I well knew was further than any boat at Para had ever gone. The baggage had been placed on board the schooner on Thursday, and it is but fair that I should tell of what that baggage was composed.

Our character of merchants was not so much assumed as we would have liked it to have been, as neither Ned nor I was, at that time, well enough off in the goods of this world to travel such a distance without carrying a 'venture' along with us. The 'venture' on this occasion was of some value, as several *real* merchants, of our acquaintance, had kindly interested themselves in *our* welfare, by consigning all sorts of things to us on commission, such as cutlery, hardware, tea, cooking utensils, a few agricultural implements, silks, satins, velvets, &c., being such articles as would sell to great advantage in Lima, Quito, or any of the cities on the Pacific side of the Andes, should we fail in obtaining admission to the valley. We had, independently of the above, some really valuable articles which Ned and I had brought from Asia in 1842; and for our own use during the travels, we carried edibles to some amount, and all of the best quality. Our personal baggage was reduced to its lowest limits, and thus provided we sailed on the Amazon, employing the time in perfecting ourselves in that most comprehensive language—the Amaquis, with which we had been previously acquainted in a slight degree.

About eleven o'clock on the morning of the Thursday following our departure from Para, we arrived at the unaccountably dirty town of Santarem, in front of which were a great many indescribable conveyances intended to float on the river. Immediately upon leaving the 'St. Joao,' we pounced upon one of these, which was the only specimen, that we saw, that had the slightest appearance of being able to stand upright, and engaged it forthwith.

We got off at five o'clock the next morning, and, considering the singular form of our conveyance, we travelled pretty rapidly over the surface of the beautiful Rio Tapajos. The wind continued in our favour all day, and about seven in the evening we passed the last settlement of any size on the river,—that is to say, the village of Aldea de Mondrucus,—and at dark entered the verge of the great interior forest of Brazil, but it was too late to see anything distinctly. Our captain told us that we should have enough of the woods before we reached Povoacao, as there was nothing else all the way, if we excepted a family or two, that had cut down a few trees, and built a house on the banks of the river,—we consequently rolled ourselves up in our cloaks and turned the after deck into a bed, where,—or on which,—we slept soundly until a little before sunrise, when the captain awoke us, and we went to the side of the boat to see all that was to be seen, which was not much, as it was nearly as dark as pitch, but we discovered that our vessel was at a stand still.

In a few moments the purple clouds, that herald the rising of the sun, appeared above the horizon, and, rapidly ascending to the zenith, were closely followed by others, of various shades of pink, and at last the sudden appearance of a globe of intense light, warned us of the day's having fairly commenced. We now found that our craft had stopped before what, in our Western states, would be called a 'clearing,' where a hut or two, built of logs, proclaimed the residence of man, in a more civilized state than is usually found in the interior of Brazil.

Almost with the sun, a tall, gawky looking genius came out of one of the cabins with a large package of skins in his hands. "That is, unmistakably, a Yankee," I whispered to Ned; "try him when he comes up." So, when the "squatter" got to the side of the boat and had, in horribly bad Spanish, consigned his bundle to the captain, that it might be taken to Povoacao, Grey called out, in English,

"Hollo, there! I guess you're a Yankee, aint you?"

The poor fellow looked quite surprised at being addressed in his native idiom, and stared at us most unmercifully, replying:—"Waal, stranger, I reckon I come from the Bay state."

"How did you get into this outlandish place?" was Ned's next query, and the squatter told us his long and miserable tale, which I will condense into the smallest space. Going on board of a whaling ship, after a long and disastrous voyage, the vessel was wrecked on the North-east coast of Australia. With some of his ship-mates he set out to walk from the wreck to the town of Sidney, where he and one other arrived after much hardship. Having resided in this settlement for a few months, he at last joined an English convict-ship, which was to return to England, touching at Rio Janeiro, as a sailor. While the ship was at Rio he deserted, having been badly treated, and hid himself until it had departed, when he applied to nearly all the United States' ships in port, none of which required his services, so he started alone, on foot for Para. In passing through the country he thought it would be a fine place to settle in. He got to Para, and found a situation on board of a schooner bound for Nahant, where he arrived in safety after a perilous passage. The next spring he brought out his family and had established himself where we had found him.

We asked him how he got on, and if he liked his "location," to which he replied: "Business is thrivin' in the skin trade, but the Injins is rayther troublesome. As to the *sitivation*, it's good enough for the landway, but as hot as ten thunders!"

We made him a present of some cutlery, which we knew would be useful to a man in his *sitivation*, although it was with a good deal of difficulty that we got him to overcome his Yankee pride and receive it, and after a long conversation, we bade farewell. Our sails were set and we once more started for Povoacao.

As our captain had told us, the banks of the river were covered with a thick forest, through which the sun could scarcely penetrate ; there was no breeze of any consequence, and we had to take to the oars, to *cool* ourselves.

CHAPTER IV.

The Navigation of the lower Tapajos.—Aground.—The Rio Arinos.—Povoacao.—The Beginning of the Journey.

ON the second day's journey we had noticed that the width of the river rapidly decreased, so what was our astonishment, on awaking on Sunday morning, to find our boat sailing over an expanse of water, at least four miles wide! It was the mouth of the Rio Azovedo, one of the largest tributaries of the Tapajos, and emptying itself into the latter from the south. About ten o'clock we came to the mouth of another stream, pouring its waters from the north, and, on my maps, without a name, but called by our captain, the Rio Urupas. At noon, or a very little after, we passed the mouth of a third stream from the south, named the Rio Cavaiva.

The Tapajos now grew gradually narrower, and at the same time more shallow, so that one of the six seamen belonging to our vessel, was constantly at the bows on the look out for sand banks, sunken rocks, and other enemies to navigation, for the lead was not required on account of the great transparency of the water.

"Labordo! labordo! vito! Labordo! Santa Maria!" suddenly exclaimed our *foreman*, while the helmsman endeavored to obey his order. But it was too late, I heard the grating noise of the sand beneath the keel (if it had one,) and we were aground! The sailors calling upon all the saints in the calendar, and more too, seized two long stout spars, which are always carried by the vessels going up and down the inland rivers of South America, and with desperate shoves and pushes, at length got our craft off.

At a little after six in the afternoon, the bows of the boat were turned directly towards the eastern shore, and I imagined that we were going straight aground for a second time, as I could see nothing but foliage. Notwithstanding appearances, nothing of the kind took place, for the mast,—being suddenly deprived of the sails,—parted the branches of the trees, and in two minutes we were resting quietly in the centre of what we travellers at first, took for a lake, but in fact it was the mouth of the Rio Arinos. The continuation of the river was invisible from our situation, and that part of it which we did see, was perfectly circular, entirely surrounded by hills of about fifty feet in height, thickly wooded from their summits to the very edge of the river, where the densely foliaged trees swept their luxuriant branches in the pure, cool, fresh water, which flowed silently to its shallow outlet, the width of which was hidden by the trees which had taken root in the damp soil, and had grown up, completing this grand natural amphitheatre. The little lake,—I must call it so,—was dotted over with small conical islands, covered with trees, and seeming like forests growing in the water.

The sails were again set, and, with a light breeze which wafted us along, we darted into the Rio Arinos.

At half past twelve on Monday, we arrived in front of Povoacao, further than which we could not have gone, if we had wished, as about a mile from the town there is a little cascade, just high enough to prevent navigation. Across the Arinos, at this town, is thrown a fragile structure, honoured by the name of bridge, but on which, I am not ashamed to own, I always felt very insecure and rather alarmed. It is, or was, *built* in the following manner. Three ropes are stretched between the banks, and on these are lashed narrow boards, exactly the width of the bridge in length, about a foot wide, and placed about eighteen inches apart. In 1830, I think, a *bridge*, similar to this, broke in half during the periodical rains, and precipitated several persons into a torrent over which it had been cast. This accident was, it is said, caused by the shrinking of the wet ropes.

Povoacao is, at the smallest computation, three hundred and forty miles from any civilized community, and but little known on the Atlantic. Indeed, I doubt very much if I could have found a vessel, at Para, whose captain was acquainted with its precise situation. It is, nevertheless, a settlement of some size, and a few of the inhabitants have immense droves of horses, mules, and other beasts of burden, and they also have extensive plantations of tropical productions, which, however, are not sufficiently well cultivated to prove very lucrative. The town has suffered severely from several attacks made upon it by the surrounding savage tribes, who appear to bear the greatest enmity towards all new settlers.

Immediately on arriving our baggage was taken out of the boat, and placed, for the time being, under the portico of a house, which, being deserted, we took the liberty of entering and establishing as our head quarters during our stay. In the afternoon I procured five horses,—for the use of ourselves and servants,—and thirty mules to carry our merchandise and baggage, which we spent all day Tuesday in dividing into packages suitable for a mule's back, leaving the empty packing cases in the house, of which we had so summarily taken possession.

Wednesday morning was the tug of war. We got up long before dawn, and, by torchlight, commenced loading our animals, which employed us fully until sunrise, when we took a slight breakfast, saddled our horses, mounted them, and set out on our journey.

We ventured to carry arms as far as the Terra Incognita, if we were to find it, and if we did do so they were such as could easily be concealed, the rifles having been made with the shortest barrels consistent with safety. Each of us, servants included, had one of those inestimable inventions know as Colt's Revolvers, and good stout bowie knives were not omitted in our accoutrements.

Crossing the ticklish bridge, we continued along the river's bank all day long, passing at three o'clock in the afternoon, the mouth of the Rio Oru, which empties itself into the Arinos from the south east, and at sunset we encamped for the night, on the edge of the forest, at the confluence of the two rivers, Sumidor and Flores, which together form that on which Povoacao is situated.

Our tents were pitched, the mules unloaded, and, with the horses, turned out to graze. Large fires were kindled around our small camp to keep away the wild animals; and after eating our supper we sank to rest, and slept without the slightest interruption until the first beams of the rising sun warned us to arise and prepare for another day's travel, which we did, and pursued our way along the western bank of the Sumidor.

CHAPTER V.

A Brazilian Forest.—A Curiosity.—A Lion monkey.—The Hills.—An Ascent.—A Supper in the dark.

Monday evening, October 4th.—The fifth day of our land journeyings is over, we having rested all yesterday on the banks of the Sumidor, where we arrived on Saturday. This morning, at sunrise, we left the river and, for the first time, entered the Brazilian Forest, through which we have been slowly forcing our way, since that time. Nothing, however, can be more beautiful than the scenery around some of the natural openings, in one of which we are now encamped. A tiny rivulet bubbles over the stony bed, with a rocky shore nearly covered with the *Lecythis* that bears the curious flower so much resembling a pitcher. Trees of every tropical variety surround this streamlet. The airy foliaged silk-tree, as it is commonly called, but which I think, botanists term *Bombax*, the trunk and branches of which, particularly the latter, are armed with long and sharp thorns; the trumpet-tree with its straight, tall stem and tufted branches, the innumerable palms, with their broad, umbrella-like summits, grow every where of every size, from the gigantic *Charita*, down to the little dwarf palm, which spreads its large thick leaves within a few inches of the ground. Then there is the glorious rosewood tree, or *jacarantha*, charming us with the richness of its enormous gold-coloured flowers, and the magnificence of its feathered leaves; the delightfully perfumed Vanilla, the delicious Tonquin bean; and the not quite so agreeable ipecacuanha and sarsaparilla. We have just been drinking some vegetable milk obtained with the assistance of my pen-knife from the very appropriately named *cow-tree*, and it is very much like animal milk, though not quite so rich. It is said to have all the qualities of the latter:—was *butter* ever made of it?

Ned's fowling piece—and mine too, for that matter,—has been popping all day at the gorgeously plumed birds: toucans, parrots, curassows, macaws, paroquets, guans, and many another of the feathered tribes have *representatives* in our game bags, forming quite a *congress*, some indeed calculated for a *provisional* government. I have one of those rarely seen curl-crested Aracari so much prized for their beautiful plumage. Ned is decidedly jealous of this possession of mine, as I am of one of his,—an equal curiosity in the shape of a *darra*, or bell bird. Unfortunately this last loses its principal charm in dying, this is to say, its voice, which has the peculiar metallic sound from which it derives its common name.

I have found M—r—e's air gun of much use in killing the lovely little humming birds, thousands of which, of every colour in the rainbow, dart about among the singularly shaped parasitical plants that cling to nearly every tree. Grey intends preserving the skins of our most beautiful birds, to take home with him and have stuffed. They will form a very valuable and scarce collection.

Wednesday evening, October 6th.—If there is to be an end of our journeyings before we reach the Pacific coast, I think that we are not now far from it, being encamped at the source of the little Rio Oteicorolla, a branch of the Rio St. Rito, the last known tributary of any size, of the Tapajos.

We face the south west, and on our left and in front of us, the serrated summits of the Sierra Paricis,—or Parexis,—rear themselves towards the sky, as we can see through the openings of the forest which is not near so thick as it has been during our last day's journey, and I think that within a few miles of where we now are, there must be either a plain or a river, but that remains to be proved, as neither are down on my miserable maps.

Throughout our travels from Povoacao we have

not seen a single wild animal, if we except the tribes of monkeys, who are wild enough in all conscience and infest the whole forest. We caught yesterday afternoon a young lion monkey otherwise called the marikina (*Midas Rosalia*), a most ridiculous caricature of his majestic godfather, being a positive daguerreotype likeness. It had a ferocious mane, and a whisking, tufted, tail. His actions and colour resembled the African Lion precisely, but the face seemed perpetually on the grin from the peculiar set of the mouth. He was less than a foot long, and we were anxious to keep and bring him home with us, but the little rascal took it into his head to make himself scarce last night and we are left quite disconsolate at his loss.

I am writing in my tent by the light of a candle, which,—in lieu of a candle stick,—is placed in 'a hole,' cut in the top of a ripe pineapple. We have had a long day's journey, and as I am proportionably tired, I shall close my journal.

On Thursday morning, the seventh of October, we did not commence our march until near nine o'clock, having been detained by a mule having strayed away. However, we found her, and set out, coming, at eleven o'clock to the edge of the woods.

Before us was spread a plain, and, at the distance of about a mile, rose a range of precipitous hills, nearly fourteen hundred feet high as we subsequently found, although, at first sight, they seemed much lower. Two immense mountains,—by comparison,—reared their hoary heads behind these hills, and still further back peeped the Sierra Paricis, blue in the distance, but becoming gradually of a more distinct colour as they swelled toward our left, which they passed, being lost to our veiw by the intervening forest. On the right they came partially up to meet the range of hills, and then retreated to their old position.

As we approached the hills, in a line towards the south east, we heard the sound of descending water, and at length saw, several miles to our right, the mist rising from a series of broad cataracts, one above the other, being altogether, about a hundred feet high. From the foot of the lowest fall ran a stream, winding its tortuous way through the plain, and losing itself in the woods. On the extreme right, at a distance of about thirty miles west-south-west of the cataracts, as well as I could judge, was one of the two high mountains above mentioned,—a towering, needle-like peak, the upper part of which was buried in snow, while below this came narrow bands of different shades of green. The other one was much lower and about the same distance due south of us:—towards it we rode, examining the hills carefully, in search of a sufficiently easy slope, as all we then saw, were nearly inaccessible for mules, letting alone the horses and ourselves.

We rode, and rode rapidly too, until our horses nearly gave out, but there was still nothing to be seen but absolute precipices. We had passed the smaller of the two tall mountains, and were just determining to call the annoying hills, the Sierra Perplex-us, in contradistinction to the neighbouring Sierra Parexis, when we discovered a gentle hill,—by comparison. It being very near sundown, and the ascent to the lowest plateau being very long, we decided upon encamping for the night at the foot of the hill, just where we were, which we did, being very much fatigued after a most tiresome ride.

We commenced the ascent at seven o'clock, and after an exceedingly dangerous and fatiguing climb, reached the first plateau from the ground, at two, having been seven hours on the hill. Between the fatigue, excitement, heat, and a good dinner, we fell asleep after having demolished the latter almost entirely, and did not rouse ourselves until long after three, when we recommenced climbing, this time for the summit, which we did not gain until the moon was shining resplendently.

When there, the tinder box could not be found,

and, as it has as yet, not been discovered what kind of lens it takes to light a fire by the ray of the moon,—we fully expected to be obliged to go to rest supperless, or nearly so, as we thought that our meal could only consist of the rather scanty remains of our dinner.

But such was not fated to be our doom, as our most excellent and thoughtful cook,—by name Harry Boyd, who with his two brothers Peter and Joseph, have accompanied Ned and I in all our many travels,—had provided, in case of accidents, an ample store of bananas, pineapples, and other fruits growing wild on the plain and in the forest, which he now produced.

We devoured them with wondrous avidity, in darkness, and in silence, all of us being much too busily engaged to talk. After this we turned in immediately, and slept like so many humming tops, not even dreaming of what we were in hopes of having the pleasure of seeing on the following morning.

CHAPTER VI.

First View of the Valley.—Encounter on the descent.—The Curaça of Ocopaltepec.

As may be supposed, all five of us were up and stirring long enough before dawn, waiting in anxiety for the rising of the "*diurnal luminary,*" as Carlyle calls it,—for we felt assured that we were near the wished-for termination of our journey. All that we could discern, by the light of the gradually fading stars, was an indistinct mass on our right, blacker than the nearly impenetrable darkness, but which, from its situation, we conjectured to be the smaller peak of the two hills.

At length, after an apparently interminable wait on our part, the first rays of the sun struck the top of this mass, and quickly descending, displayed the mountain, terraced from its summit to the ground, as we could easily see even at the distance we were from it. In a moment more we found that we were standing on the eastern boundary of a valley, surrounded, on a little more than two of its sides, by the towering, heaven-threatening mountains of the Sierra Paricis, while the remainder was compassed in by the hills we had seen two days before. The level of the valley was closely covered with fortified cities, walled and unwalled towns and villages,* connected with each other by stone causeways, lined, on either side, with rows of trees. Not far from the foot of the mountain on which we were, stood a large walled town, whose white buildings glistened in the sun's rays, and the mountain itself was terraced more than three-fourths of the way up, thickly strewn with hamlets and the residences of the owners or tenants, and of the labourers on the plantations, which last glowed with all kinds of vegetation,—from the golden wheat of the north, which was flourishing on the upper terrace, and which,—being moved by the morning's cool and gentle zephyrs,—seemed to bow to the newly risen orb of day, bending its bearded heads as if in humble adoration of that Great Being who had sent the refreshing air,—down to the stately groves of banana, jatropha,

* I must here mention that on the map, which forms the frontispiece of this book,—I have only placed those cities, towns, &c., which I have actually visited, and of which I happen to know the names and situations. By the native maps,—which I subsequently saw,—it appears that there are more than twice as many towns as I had put down. Notwithstanding this, I have left the map in its original state, and thus it makes its appearance.

and cocoa, growing on the level of the valley, and seeming to triumph in the protection of a just Providence.

As the day became more advanced, the houses gave up their occupants, who trooped to their work through the luxuriant fields:—at the height which we were above them, they looked more like ants than men.

Our view on the north west was bounded by the tallest of the two peaks, and terminated, in all other directions, by the misty-blue, undefined mountains of the Sierra Paricis. On the extreme south-western corner of the valley we could indistinctly see an immense fortified city, the largest in view, and which we immediately fixed upon as the capital.

No! there was not the slightest doubt about it—we had found the VALLEY OF GERAL!—but we had not entered it. This last had now to be attempted, and as a premonitory symptom of our intention to do so, all our weapons and firearms were concealed with the greatest care, and loading our mules, we mounted our horses, and commenced the descent of the fertile Sierra, which rolled down gracefully and gradually; in every respect the very opposite of its other side, where nearly perpendicular cliffs combatted for supremacy with unmistakably sterile slopes.

We descended toward the south-west in the direction of the large town, near the base of the mountain, and before we reached the wheat plateau, encountered an immense herd of llamas, attended by twenty or thirty natives. These last, on seeing us, took to their heels, and all but flew down the terraces, closely followed by their gentle and pretty charges. This annoyed us, as we had wished to make friends with them, so that we might give them to understand our amicable intentions. In order to overtake them, Ned and I put spurs to our horses, and, leaving the mules in the care of the servants that they might be made to follow us down to the valley, we galloped after the fleeing *llamaherds*.

This was easier said than done, for our steeds, not having been trained to walk up and down stairs, could not descend the short flights which connected the terraces, without exposing their riders to the danger of their relative positions being reversed; that is to say, the horse on top of the man. As we did not think this would be as agreeable as the usual method of riding, we gave up all idea of catching the fugitives, and, dismounting, led the animals. The servants and mules soon joined us, the former leading their horses, and the latter descending without the slightest difficulty. As we went on we saw several parties of labourers, but on our approach they all fled, and we pursued our course uninterruptedly until eleven o'clock, about which hour we gained the second terrace from the ground.

Here we were rather surprised to find a large body of warriors, drawn up so as to prevent our further progress, and armed with bows and arrows, lances, javelins, slings, and other barbarian weapons, and also carrying numerous banners with different devices on them. Those whom we singled out as chieftains were assembled, in front of the army, around a low litter of a reddish coloured wood inlaid with mother of pearl and gold. As we came near, the curtains of this conveyance were opened, and there descended a person evidently *somebody*, attired in a superb dress. A rim of gold,—ornamented with pendant jewels of great value, and decorated with an aigrette, composed of the feathers of the rhea, or American ostrich, dyed scarlet,—encircled his head; over his shoulders was a mantle of peculiar form, somewhat resembling a poncho, save that it was of even length all around, and had holes for the arms to come through,—it fell nearly to his knees, and was made of some thick white stuff, richly embroidered with gold cross-bars, and bordered with scarlet; his feet were defended by sandals, with gold soles, and having the leathern straps bossed with the same metal. He was about twenty-seven years of age, nearly six feet tall, and had a very prepossessing expression of countenance.

As he descended, all the attendant chiefs touched, with their right hand, first their forehead and then the ground. Seeing that he approached us, we all halted and awaited his arrival. He came on quickly, attended by the chieftains, and when immediately before us, at a distance of about five feet, they all stopped short. A chief, who stood by the side of the principal person, now addressed us in Amaquis, which speech, although it loses much by its bad translation, I give in full, as it was as curt as you please.

"Cioaco, the brave and mighty Curaça of Ocopaltepec, demands in the name of Orteguilla, the Inca, our father, and the Child of the Sun, why the strangers have dared to enter the Geral-milco without asking the consent of our father the Inca?"

"We come," I answered, "from the far north to sell our goods in the city of the Inca, and we bring presents to him." "How do we know but that you come as enemies?" asked a ferocious looking gentleman behind the Curaça. "If we were enemies would there not be more of us?" I asked; "and since when have enemies brought presents? Do not enemies come with bows and spears?" This was unanswerable, and Ned, taking my hint, went to extract a present from the load of one of the mules, while I kept up the conversation. In a moment Grey reappeared bearing in his arms a roll of mazarine blue silk,—not out of *my* goods,—and an axe. When I saw the last I felt afraid the Curaça's opinion of our being enemies might return on seeing us armed with such a formidable looking weapon, but when I presented them to him, they were received with evident admiration, and it was clear that we were considered as friends now. He returned most of his thanks with his fine eyes, as he said but little, and the other spokesman, after conferring with him for a short time, told us to accompany Cioaco's escort to the nearest town, where he would leave us, while he went on to the Inca to request admission in our name.

The Curaça then entered his litter and descended the two terraces, closely followed by our party. When we got to the level of the valley, and on a broad stone causeway, we mounted our horses, to the great fright of the *army*, who had never seen such big four legged animals before.

At three o'clock we arrived at the walled town to which we had originally intended to direct our steps, but ourselves and beasts were not permitted to enter the gates. Consequently we encamped where we were, and settled ourselves down to await the arrival of a message from the Inca, our tents being strictly guarded by a number of warriors under a chief named Mixtecaltzin.

CHAPTER VII.

Departure from Quauhtitlan.—Ocopal.—Colucatl.—The Mexican Character of Names.—Night View from the Fortress.

At four o'clock on Sunday morning, October 10th, 1847, we were awakened by the arrival of the Inca's answer, which was immediately communicated to us by Mixtecaltzin, and as it may be considered a curiosity, I insert the translation.

"*To the Strangers at Quauhtitlan:—*

"The Inca Orteguilla, Child of the Sun and Moon, the Brother of the Stars, orders them to come, on receiving this, to his city. He commands their escort to keep them from entering the towns, as the strange creatures they have with them may hurt the townsmen. He has a house for them, meat for them, a stall in the Market Place for their goods, and room for their presents. Let them haste.

"In the name of the Inca,

"Apixtamatl Huaxteuctli."

This document* is in Amaquis of course, and is inscribed upon paper, made from the inner bark of the cocoa-tree, in coloured hieroglyphics.

In obedience to the command it contained, we commenced preparing for instant departure from Quauhtitlan, and at five o'clock started, accompanied by the same escort, who were horridly afraid of our horses and mules. We were, of course, obliged to rein in the former to a walk so that the warriors might keep up with us, and in this manner we poked along until ten o'clock when we got to a town, the name of which I found was Ocopal. Although it was unwalled we were not permitted to enter, but were left, about half a mile from it, to eat and refresh ourselves.

After eleven we set out again with a new escort but the same chief, and at three halted once more for a change of warriors outside the town of Colucatl, which, being situated upon a rising ground, afforded a very good view of the large walled city, mentioned in the last chapter, as occupying the south-western corner of the valley, —and I could see that it partially enclosed a good-sized lake, and that the walls,—of great height,—

* As the reader may suppose, it is still in my possession, and is carefully kept.

encompassed parts of the plateaus of the surrounding mountains.

We had travelled all the way from Quauhtitlan over stone causeways, bordered by rows of trees, and almost lined with houses and gardens, the plantations being almost exclusively confined to the terraces of the mountains. Our warriors were not ready to accompany us until after four o'clock, when we left Colucatl, proceeding in a direction nearly due west, a very little deviating towards the south.

What had surprised me most during our first day in the valley was the great prevalence of Mexican names, for I had heard but three that bore the slightest resemblance to those attributed to the Peruvians,—viz., Orteguilla, the name of the Inca; Cioaco, that of the friendly Curaça; and Geral, the appellation of the valley. But this last was un-Peruvianized by means of the Astecan addition of 'milco,' meaning valley. The name of the chief of our escort,—Mixtecaltzin, and those of two of the towns through which we had passed,—Quauhtitlan and Colucatl,—presented the three characteristic, consonantal, terminations of the northern language.

At twenty minutes past six, our party halted at the town of Ameralqua, on the banks of the lake,—which I now learnt was called Naloma,—

where, Ned, I, and the servants, took our suppers. The Lake was not only ornamented with four, real fortified islands, but with innumerable little floating fellows, called by the ancient inhabitants of Tenochtitlan, Chinampas, so I was not at all astonished to hear them so termed by our escort. From the town to the nearest of the island forts, there ran a strong dyke,—or more properly bridge, as the water passed through numerous triangular openings,—and we saw that the isles themselves were connected with each other in the same manner, and also, that the one nearest the city was joined to it by three remarkably broad ones, two of which appeared to be a continuation of the walls encompassing the capital.

The town end of the dike of Ameralqua was defended by two fortresses of great height and strength, and the sun had not yet set,—although it was nearly half past seven,—when we passed between them and got on the dike.

We had nearly reached the first island when Mixtecaltzin, cried out,—"Hasten! Oh warriors! Our Master is bidding farewell to the summit of the mountain of Atola! Hasten, or the gates of the fortress will be closed." The men walked faster, and Ned and I put our horses in a gallop, much to the fear of the escort, who crowded to one side of the dike that we might pass on.

As the last man entered the fortress, the sun set, and the gates clanged together behind us—and before us too, which was more than we bargained for. That we should have to spend the night where we were, was plainly evident, and in consequence we selected a camping *ground* upon the stone court-yard, where the animals were now driven, fastened and unloaded. This done, Ned and I ascended to the top of the walls to see what was to be seen, and there undoubtedly was something very well worth seeing.

Athough the sun had not been down an hour, it was dark as midnight, there being as yet no moon, and the stars not having so soon attained their greatest brilliancy. The grey unilluminated, jagged walls of the three other island fortresses were immediately before us, accidentally so placed as to form what appeared from our situation to be a barrier across the lake. Beyond these the Sierra Paricis could just be discerned from its greater darkness than the sky, and also by its many summits having already received, on their eastern sides, the first rays of the moon, as yet invisible in the less elevated parts of the valley. As we gazed on this singular scene a change suddenly came over it, rendering it even more remarkable. A brilliant, but flickering red light at once illuminated the lower plateaus of the Sierra, and this being lost in the foliage of higher terraces had a peculiar and mysterious effect. Nearest to us were the now apparently coal-black walls of the forts, immediately above them glowed the fiery light melting into impenetrable darkness, over which gleamed the snow-capped moon-lit summits of the mountains.

After regarding this magnificent coup d'œil for some time, we inquired the cause of the red flickering light, and learnt that it was produced by fires kindled on the roof of every house in Geral on the rising of the moon whenever that took place. As the heavenly lamp of night rose higher and higher, the fires one by one died out, but the native of whom we inquired, told us that on those nights when the 'Mother of the Inca,' —as they call the moon,—did not appear, the fires were kept up until daybreak.

We retired to rest at ten o'clock, having been notified to the effect that we should have to start on the first glimpse of the sun.

CHAPTER VIII.

A mistake.—First View of the Capital.—Reception at the Gates.

In pursuance of the orders communicated to us, we were ready to start at dawn, but as the gates of the fortress could not be opened until sunrise, we were obliged to await that event. In the meantime we fished our way, in the darkness, to a gate, leading as we thought to the dike connecting the island, on which we were, with the next in order towards the city, and here we seated ourselves, wondering why we were not joined by our escort. The sun soon made his appearance over the eastern mountains, and the gates were thrown open by the officials. We were about to pass through at once, alone, and should have done so, had not Grey taken a peep first and found out that we were at the wrong dike, as this one led to the shores of the lake, although it was not that by which we had entered the fortress on the previous night.

As we stood still, wondering what we should do next, we were relieved by the appearance of

Mixtecaltzin, who had, we found, been searching for us every where. He told us that this was a dike leading to a little town named Onadella, on the west bank of the lake, and added that the men awaited us at another gate, whither we immediately followed him, the horses and mules being led by the servants. We were soon on the proper dike, and in a short time passed through the three other fortresses, entering, from the last one, on the middle of the three bridges leading to the city, it being the shortest and also the broadest, as the greater part of the others was occupied by the walls of the city which connected the banks of the lake and the island forts by means of the two dikes.

Crowds of people swarmed on the bridge we crossed,—although we obtained an easy passage from their fear of our animals,—and the lake was a mass of canoes filled with natives. At the end of the dike frowned a high, stone, fortified building with a wide entrance, evidently one of the city gates.

I chanced to look towards my left, and I saw the capital. Being built on a gradually rising ground, a plan of it might almost have been drawn from where I was. In some parts, monstrously broad streets, flanked by large houses of white stone with flat roofs, with gardens around them,—ran from the foot of the Sierra Paricis to the very edge of the lake, in perfectly straight lines. Hundreds of elevated buildings,—probably temples, towered over the city, which was diversified with immense parks, or enclosures filled with trees.

We moved on but slowly through the dense crowd, and passed through the dike gate. As we entered this strong fortress, our ears were shocked by a sudden burst of savage and discordant *music*,—it was the Inca's band,—and in a few moments he and his cortege came in sight. A more gorgeous display I never saw.

The procession was opened by a throng of military officers in their magnificent costumes. On their heads they wore helmets formed like the heads of various wild animals, composed of silver, gold, or bronze, ornamented,—rather singularly, and, according to my ideas, very inappropriately,—with crests of feathers and jewels. Cuirasses,—made of either of the three above named metals, but invariably wrought like the scales of a fish,—were placed over their breasts, with kelts, of different materials, falling from their lower edge, reaching nearly to the knee. On their shoulders, and hanging down their backs, were fastened cloaks either of stained or embroidered cotton cloth, or of feather work. A few of the most renowned warriors, I suppose, wore the skins of wild beasts, the head resting on the helmet, and the fore paws falling over the shoulders. All of these chieftains were armed with different kinds of weapons.

Next came the band,—not *par excellence,*—consisting of a great many natives making a most horrific noise upon reed flutes, wooden trumpets, snakeskin drums, conches, and other barbarous inventions intended to discourse most excruciating music. After these came a large number of nobles, probably those holding high offices of state. They wore dresses like that which Cioaco had on during our interview on the terrace of the little sierra. Carried on the shoulders of sixteen of these magnificently attired gentlemen, was an open litter, composed of gold, superbly wrought, bossed with precious stones and inlaid with mother of pearl, having a canopy of the feathers of the Rhea, dyed in various colours. In this was seated the Inca, Orteguilla, wearing the *llautu,* the sacred *borla,* and the military dress of an officer of high rank, it being composed of a golden ciruass bossed with silver, and studded with gems, golden sandals, similarly decorated, the skin of a jaguar served for a cloak, and a kelt of green *plumaje.* The crimson fringe of the borla fell almost in his eyes, giving a most singular expression to an otherwise strikingly handsome face, his features being regular and his complexion of a clear, although dark, olive. His eyes were remarkably fine, and had an exceedingly benevolent and engaging expression. I should not think that he was over forty, if so much. His only disfigurement was in his ears, which having been cut, according to '*fashion*,' for the insertion of large, jewelled balls of gold,—the insignia of royal birth,—had gradually been pulled down by the weight of these cumbrous articles, until they rested on his shoulders; but they were a good deal hidden by his hair, which was,—as indeed was that of every noble present,—excessively long and curling in ringlets.

On seeing us, he motioned the procession to stop, and, descending from his litter, approached us, followed closely by the nobles, while Ned and I advanced to meet him.

Then commenced an interchange of compliments, in the course of which we ascertained, with considerable difficulty, that we were welcome to Geral, that the city was open to us, and that a palace had been prepared for our reception. Having spun this little information out,—in the manner of some modern novelists,—as the subject of at least ten minutes conversation, the Inca retired to his litter and from the fortress, attended

RICHARDSON-COX, SC. N.Y.

by the same retinue, with the exception of two nobles whom he left behind him to conduct us to *our* palace;—their names were Conatzin and Oradalda.

We followed them through several broad streets, filled with people,—although it was very early in the morning,—and ornamented with many splendid public buildings and equally handsome private residences, until we got to the Great Market Place, or *Tianguez*, as the Mexicans *called* it, and the Geralians *call* it, which is precisely the same thing.

Here we dismounted,—for on entering the city we had placed ourselves in the saddle, in order to have a better view of it,—and led our horses across this vast enclosure, as we were fearful that they might injure some of the many natives, who were already afraid of them, and the place was thronged with the buying and selling part of the population.

Still under the guidance of the two fine-looking and courteous chiefs, we entered an extravagantly broad thoroughfare, at the end of which, was pointed out to our notice, the immense park, and palace intended for our occupation.

CHAPTER IX.

Description of the Park and Palace.

We soon entered the gilt-gates of the large park which encircled the building, and rode up a broad avenue leading to the great entrance, where we found a crowd of native servants who had been sent to wait on us by the Inca. Here we alighted and immediately commenced hunting for an out building suitable for a stable, which Ned soon found at a short distance in the rear of the palace, and the animals were taken there as soon as the servants had unloaded the mules and had placed the packs in the large hall. This being done, and a slight breakfast having been despatched, Ned and I, under the guidance of one of the numerous attendants in the palace, took a survey of our new domicile.

As I have before mentioned, it was surrounded by a large park, which we subsequently found to contain a little over two hundred acres, filled with beds of gorgeous flowers, fountains, pavilions, shrubberies and groves of trees, and also containing an extensive aviary, which I might almost call a natural one, as it was formed only by a net, of very fine mesh, thrown over the tops of several trees, and securely fastened to the ground. Here and there through the luxuriant foliage might be seen the glittering of the sun on the large artificial lakes intended for bathing.

The palace was of grey stone, one story high, with a flat roof, or *azotea*, as the Spaniards would call it; its length was fifteen hundred feet, and the depth nine hundred, the height being thirty two. The roof was reached by two exterior flights of steps, placed in front of the building, in such a manner as to divide the façade into three equal parts, and they were each eighty feet broad consisting of fifty one steps, each step being eight inches high and fourteen deep; thus making the distance between the front of the lowest step, and the façade of the palace, fifty nine feet, six inches. On either side of these flights were two monstrous serpents carved, with a good deal of skill, out of white marble, to serve as banisters. The heads of these four snakes rested on the ground at the foot of the steps, and their widely distended mouths, ferocious looking teeth, and lolling-out tongues, had an exceedingly curious, not to say frightful, effect. The length of their upper jaws, from the corner of the mouth to the tip of the nose, was thirteen feet eight inches, and there was sufficient space between the two jaws for a seven-footer to stand, with ease. This will give an idea of their appearance.

Although the palace was, as I mentioned before, but one story in height, from the outside it looked as if it were two; for at a distance of twelve feet from the ground there projected a cornice, and above this the building ascended eighteen feet, not, however, on the same line as the portion below the cornice, but eight or nine feet further back. Beneath the cornice, the building was composed of oblong blocks of granite, of equal size, and much resembling what is called *rustic work* in architecture, it being unhewn, and only smooth for about two inches on each side of the seams. But the false story was a mass of magnificent decoration, abounding in lattice work, of stone, of the most beautiful description and carving, in which last I noticed, figuring conspicuously, the ornament so generally known as the 'Grecian border.' The corners of this second part were rounded and most grotesquely carved, with large oblongs, in which scrolls were so arranged as to represent the human face, the nose being imaged by a most curious and fanciful projection, about as much like what it was intended for, as a chandelier would be. Those parts of the façade, where the three entrances were placed, were sunk back about twenty feet, and the corners of these recesses were also rounded and adorned as above described.

The principal entrance was between the two flights of steps, and was an opening, twelve feet high by ten wide, with a gate of gilt bronze, and this admitted you into a very broad hall, paved with marble, leading to a large circular court in the centre of the building. On both sides of this were apertures, having draperies of different colours hanging over them to serve as doors. I will here mention that the court yard received three other halls,—like that which I am about to describe,—one leading from the back, and the other two from either end of the structure.

Our guide moved aside the drapery of the first door on the right, as we entered the hall, and we stood in a spacious apartment, about 100 feet square. At a distance of twenty feet from the walls rose a square of porphyry columns,—closely resembling in form those of the East Indian temples, being of a vase-like shape, standing on a tall pedestal, with a capital somewhat resembling a compressed cushion,—richly carved, and supporting a balustrade which surrounded an opening in the roof, through which a flood of light poured down on a small fountain which bubbled in the centre of the room. The walls were hung with a pale sea-green tapestry, embroidered with gold flowers, and the piles of cushions, of all shapes and sizes, that were thrown over the marble floor, were of the same colour and style.

Another piece of tapestry was raised by our guide, and admitted us into a hall, which we crossed and entered a second room much larger than the first, but of similar construction. The colour which principally attracted the eye, however, was not as agreeable, being a sickly, sulphureous yellow. Leaving this ghostly room as quickly as possible, we passed through several small apartments, until we came to a narrow entry, which, we were told, was made in the northern wall of the palace, and along this we walked for some distance, till, at last, we came to a granite wall, forming the termination of the entry:—on our left was a hanging. It was raised and we entered an apartment, long and narrow,—by comparison. Two sky-lights,—if I may so call them,—afforded the only illumination of this saloon, which was hung with gray tapestry, looped up so as to display an underhanging of buff embroidered with silver. The floor was of highly polished marble, and the ceiling of carved rose-wood. The cushions in this room were of gray and silver.

Not to fatigue the reader, I will describe but

one room more,—my chamber, which was situated on the southern side of the central hall, and entered by passing through two smaller apartments, handsomely furnished, and appropriated to my particular use. On seeing this apartment, both Ned and I decided upon its being the most splendid in the palace.

It was sixty-five feet long, forty wide, and twenty-five high, with the usual square of porphyry columns in the centre, here enclosing a space of twenty feet, in the middle of which was a fountain. The ceiling was of cedar, covered with very delicately carved foliage; the floor was only visible within the square of the columns, where it was composed of differently coloured woods, so put together as to form a pattern; the other and greater portion was raised three steps higher than that around the fountain, and was covered with a thick, velvety looking, creamish-coloured material, embroidered all over with large bouquets of flowers, so beautifully done, as to seem like real ones.

The walls were draped with scarlet tapestry embroidered with gold cross-bars, having a circle of silver in the centre of each square, and a very deep, rich border of gold flowers. These hangings fell from a gilt cornice, that ran around the top of three of the walls; but on the left hand side, as you entered, the tapestry only fell fourteen feet, for at that height from the floor, the false second story protruded into the apartment, seeming like one of those galleries so often met with in the old manor houses of merry England. Through the lattice work of this intrusion the sun was permitted to pour his rays, it being undraped.

At the end of the room, opposite the entrance, was what served for a bed;—consisting of a white cushion,—or rather, ottoman,—starred with gold, seven or eight feet square, two feet high, and plentifully provided with small cushions. It stood under a canopy of feather-work, raised twenty feet from the floor, supported in front by two slender silver columns, and, on the back wall, falling to the floor. Above the back of the canopy was a huge silver circle surrounded with small silver stars, and in each corner of the room stood an incense table, of gold, magnificently chased, and furnished with vases, and caskets of incense. The rest of the furniture consisted of stools and tables, elaborately carved out of solid blocks of ebony, cedar, rosewood, and other woods, highly polished, and the former having crimson cushions.

I will end this chapter by describing the circular court in the centre of the palace. This extensive opening had a diameter of four hundred and thirty odd feet, and was surrounded by a portico supported by a double row of the tall, vase-like pillars, before spoken of. In the centre of the enclosed space was a large and fine fountain, and four others were at equal distances around it. The whole court was paved with white marble of the purest quality, interrupted, here and there, by large beds of the most fragrant flowers of the tropics, very carefully tended by the multitude of gardeners who were attached to the large retinue of the Inca.

This, I hope, will give a slight idea of the magnificence in the midst of which we now, so unexpectedly, found ourselves placed; for we had never even dreamt of falling in with such splendour when we left Charleston.

It must not be imagined that I ascertained all the measurements given in the course of this chapter in the first day's examination of the palace, as such is not the fact. They were made long afterwards, but I thought best to insert them with the preceding description.

CHAPTER X.

Dinner.—A Promenade.—The Court of Justice.—Tianguez—The Close of the first day.

WE did not complete our explorations of the Palace until nearly twelve o'clock, but having, at last finished, we set to work. That is to say, we removed,—by the help of the natives, and our own servants,—all our merchandise into one of the numerous unoccupied rooms, and all our private baggage was placed in our separate apartments, which were in a row, side by side, mine being next to the outer wall, Ned's next, then those of our three attendants. This engaged us fully until two o'clock, a little after which hour, a native servant entered the saloon where we were, and,—understanding his low salute,—we followed him through several apartments which we had not before seen.

He raised a piece of tapestry, and admitted us into a long room, hung with light blue drapery, embroidered in silver, and lighted by three skylights. Under the middle one of these there was no fountain, but in its place stood a good sized table, with five couches around it. The table was covered with a white cotton cloth, having a deep border of silver embroidery, and laid out with a mass of gold plate, while before each guest was placed a tall silver goblet, containing a very singular and questionable looking concoction which neither Ned nor I were, at first, very anxious to taste. At last Grey,—invariably the first in every novel and dangerous adventure,—resolutely seized that before him, looked at the contents, made a wry face, but, nevertheless, put it to his lips, cautiously. One gentle sip,—a look of surprise, and an exclamation, were rapidly followed by a vacuum in the goblet, while I was recommended to try it. I did so, and found it good. It was a celebrated beverage of the ancient Peruvians and Mexicans, and called by the latter 'Chocolatl,' being a preparation of Cocoa, flavoured with vanilla, and beaten up to a froth, in which latter state it was cooled and drunk freely of during the day.*

* It is Bernal Diaz who,—in his *veritable* history of the Conquest of Mexico,—states that Montezumà had a quantity, amounting to nearly four gallons, of this beverage prepared for his own private, *daily*, consumption! But as the valiant *Conquistador*, above named, is generally believed to have been talented in the art of *drawing the long bow*, in more senses than one, we will take his *moderate* estimate at *one fourth*, and try

The dishes on the board were mostly vegetable; and besides these we had parched maize; a mixture like soup, but strongly flavoured with orange juice; tortillas, or something very much resembling them; and boiled fish. The baked flesh of the llama also appeared conspicuously, flanked by birds,—likewise baked,—such as guans, curassows, the Cancroma Cochlearca, (or boat-bill,) and others, whose names I was not acquainted with. The first two were unexceptionably fine, and were the most delicately flavoured fowls I ever ate, but the third had a slightly fishy taste which was not precisely agreeable.

We brought our own knives and forks to the table, but the former were already supplied by ones made of itzli, and the latter were supplanted by sharp pointed rods of gold. By each plate was a square piece of stuff, answering as a napkin, righly embroidered with gold and also with stained porcupine quills, which latter mode of ornamentation was rather inconvenient, and might have been dispensed with.

The first course having been demolished, the

our best to credit that the unfortunate monarch, in question, drank *one* gallon a day; and, if true, he must have had wonderfully great swallowing capacities. The drink, however, is exquisite, tasting somewhat like harlequin ice cream in a melted state.

whole table service was cleared away, even to the cloth, nothing being left but the napkins. While a clean cloth was being put on, and silver plates given to each diner, servants came to each of us with silver basins, filled with perfumed water, in which to wash our hands, they being wiped on the napkins, which were now removed, and replaced by others of scarlet and blue cotton, something like our d'Oyleys, but deeply fringed with intermingled threads of gold and silver.

Fruits were now placed on the table; bananas, pine apples, lemons, citrons, oranges, &c.; and here another singular beverage appeared, of a perfectly white colour, being composed of milk from the cow tree, flavoured with pine apple juice, and sweetened by being stirred with fresh sugar cane. Pulque was on the board in silver vases of very graceful forms, but I do not think any of us touched it. I know that I would not taste it on any account, having done so, once, in Vera Cruz. The repast ended with a second goblet of chocolatl, which none now hesitated about draining.

Not long after dinner, we received a visit from an individual, who announced himself as Palayna, an officer of the Inca's household, who had been sent to take us to the Tianguez, that we might select a stall for the sale of our merchandize.

We acknowledged Orteguilla's kindness, notwithstanding that we thought him to be rather premature,—and set out with his messenger, for the market place.

On the way to it we passed several small, but magnificent palaces, surrounded by large gardens,—which, Palayna informed us, were the residences of the higher officers of state, and the street was named, that of the Nobles. After a much longer walk than we had bargained for, the street opened into the Tianguez. On our left rose a majestic edifice, composed of three stories, each succeeding one being smaller than the last, so that the flat roof of the lowest formed a terrace around the second, and so on, while the separate stories were reached by an immense flight of steps. Our guide told us that this was the Court of Justice belonging to the Tianguez, and accompanied us into it, where we were received by three natives, dressed in long blue robes, whom we conjectured to be the judges. Nor were we wrong, for we had not been in the building five minutes, when a crowd of natives rushed in, having in their midst a man, who, from his dress, we knew to be a vendor in the Tianguez. All those who had come in began to accuse him,—with amazing volubility,—of having sold some bad fruit, which was brought in to prove their assertion. The judges soon despatched the case by making the prisoner eat the fruit, which he did with much distaste, and then went away, after leaving some money on a table. This money consisted of plates of silver about as thick as a quarter of a dollar, and nearly three quarters of an inch square, perfectly plain and having a small round hole in the centre. I should think that one was worth about thirty two cents. One of the judges told me that it was called an ochol, and that there were others of bronze and gold; one of the latter he showed me. It was much smaller than the silver one, although of the same shape.* He appeared much surprised at my never having seen one before, and asked what

* I subsequently found that, by weight, a gold ochol was worth $3 and nearly twenty-five cents; but there is another way, and, in my opinion, a fairer one, of computing the commercial value of foreign coins;—that by comparison through the medium of a commodity common to both countries. A gold ochol will purchase 4 nailles of wheat, one of which is equal to four and a half of our bushels. To-day in Philadelphia (August 2nd, 1849) white wheat is selling for $1.12½; consequently an ochol would be worth $20.25 to-day.

A silver ochol is,—by a similar computation,—equal to $3.37½, as six of them make a gold one; and one of bronze,—ten making a silver ochol,—is of value to the amount of thirty-three cents, seven mills and a half, which is near enough to say thirty-four cents.

they used in the north; so I took out my purse and showed him some of our coins, of each of which I fortunately had a specimen. The three, and Palayna, looked at them with great curiosity, and much admired the eagles on the reverse of the coins. Ned mystified them by displaying a gold Brazilian Johannes, which he happened to have with him,—and by telling that it was the principal coin of the country in which they lived. Of course they could not understand that, but they examined and highly praised its beauty, which I never could find out, with all my superior civilization.

We conversed, for some time, about matters and things in our respective nations, and at last took leave, entering the Tianguez.* This immense inclosure is entirely surrounded by a very low piazza, forty feet wide and only seven high, supported by four rows of granite piers about two feet square, dividing it into stalls twelve feet broad.† In these stalls were displayed all the different products and manufactures of the valley, while around the fountains in the

* By subsequent measurement, I found it to be one mile and nearly a half long by an average width of half a mile. It is exceedingly irregular in its form, although those which I saw in other cities were perfectly square and much smaller.

† See Appendix Number one.

centre were large droves of llamas, viçunas, &c., secured in their folds and tended by their herdsmen. In the southeastern portion of the Tianguez a great many stalls were occupied as workshops for the manufacture of chairs, tables, and other wooden articles, and others as stone cutting establishments, which operation was most laboriously undertaken with tools of a bronze composed of copper with an alloy of tin.

After walking all the way round the crowded place, we selected a stall on the northern side, and set out on our return to the palace. Palayna told us that, notwithstanding the enormous size of the market-place, there were two others within the walls of the city; a large circular one near the banks of the lake of Coxxoc, and the other, much smaller, six miles to the east of the one in which we then were. Besides these, he said there were two streets entirely appropriated to stalls and warehouses, together with factories, one of which was called the 'Street of Factories,' and the other the 'Street of the Colucatltepec.'

We soon got *home*, and Palayna took his leave, not, however, before announcing that the Inca would give us an audience the next morning, and dropping a few hints in regard to the presents which would be expected from us.

As soon as he was off, we began unpacking our bales to see what we had fit for a present to so 'great and distinguished' a personage as an Inca, and fortunately were able to decide before supper, which was served at eight, and which I have reason to expect, was a meal we introduced for the first time into the valley. As we now knew the way to the dining room, we proceeded there, and found it brilliantly illuminated by numerous golden candelabras, supporting large terra-cotta cups filled with some sort of burning fluid highly perfumed with orange. The supper itself was nearly such as we had eaten every night during our journey, with the important exception of the gold service, the tortillas, and the Chocolatl, which again made its appearance in the same way as it had at dinner.

Having partaken of this, we ascended to the flat roof, where we enjoyed a fine panoramic view of the city, first by the singular effect of the fires, and then, by moonlight—after which we walked about in the park until after ten, when we went into our chambers.

I found mine lit up with hanging lamps, one between every column around the fountain. That night I slept soundly, and so closed the first day in the city of Geral,—Monday, October 11th.

CHAPTER XI.

The Audience.—Exchange of presents.—An Afternoon's Ramble in Search of Sights.—The Streets.

TUESDAY, October 12th.—I did not hurry myself about rising this morning and,—although, by the force of habit, I awoke before dawn,—I put myself to sleep again by rejoicing that there was nothing to prevent me from so doing. O! it was delightful! and I positively believe that I was more refreshed by those three hours of extra snoosing, than I had been by all the rest of the night. However, at seven, I roused myself, and after bathing at the cool fountain, dressed and left my chamber, at the entrance of which I met Ned who was coming to see if I was sick, from having slept so much longer than usual.

After we had breakfasted, he and I put the presents for Orteguilla on a mule, and, saddling our horses, went to make ourselves spruce for the audience. At half past ten or thereabouts, the gates of the park gave admittance to Onalpo, —an officer of the house-hold, bearing a long

Peruvian word as a title, the exact interpretation of which is Lord of the Gates,—who had been sent with a goodly train of attendants, by the Inca, to conduct us to the royal palace, Orteguilla having sense enough to know that we could not find the way ourselves. Ned and I mounted and started at eleven o'clock, with Peter and the mule behind us, and surrounded by a number of Onalpo's attendants.

After a ride of over two miles, we entered the gates of a park, and found ourselves before the Inca Palace, which is, at least, sixty feet high, although consisting of but one story,—and of monstrous size. But what struck me as singular, directly I approached the building, was that the front only is of stone, the sides and outbuildings being of wood. It has four large staircases in front, which strongly resembles that of the Palace we occupy. I had not much time or opportunity to examine it this morning, as we merely went towards, not along, the side. It is very different from *ours* in one particular, and that is, that it stands on a terrace, raised four or five feet from the ground, and ascended to, by means of a flight of very steep steps, at the foot of which we were obliged to leave the horses, but brought muley with us. The terrace was covered with natives in their peace costumes, glittering with precious stones and metals, but they moved aside so as to form an alley for us to pass through, actuated—I expect,—more by a fear of the mule than by a wish to please us.

We first entered a large hall, were Onalpo slipped off his sandals, covered his handsome dress with a long black robe, and strapping a small bundle on his back, signified his readiness to conduct us to the Inca. Seeing us to be all impatience, he lifted a heavy drapery, and we found ourselves on the threshold of a broad, and exceedingly lengthy saloon, with two rows of gilt columns running the whole length of it, and lit by the immense lattices in each wall, partially shaded by hangings of light blue, sprinkled with small golden suns. The ceiling is of carved rosewood, and the floor, between the ranges of columns, is covered with a carpet like that in my chamber, while, between the columns and the wall, it is composed of different coloured marbles, as well as I could see, from the immense number of black-robed nobles standing there. At the end of the room, opposite to that at which we entered, is the throne of the Inca, the canopy over which is composed of crimson,—so richly embroidered with gold and jewels that the ground can scarcely be seen,—and it falls, in graceful folds, on either side of the chair of state,—from a golden sun, suspended some distance above the throne. The throne, itself, stands on a long dais, covered with white cloth embroidered with silver,—and is a gold stool, with a large sun behind it.

On this sat Orteguilla, with the llautu, borla, and the sacred robe of blue resplendent with jewels of great value. He was surrounded by all the high officers of the realm, in black robes, unsandled, and *bebundled*,—among whom I easily recognised the Curaça of Ocopaltepec.

We left the mule at the door under Pete's charge and entered. On seeing us, the Inca descended from his throne, and, advancing to meet us, did so about the middle of the room, whence he conducted us to the dais, where seats had been provided for Ned and I. We conversed for more than an hour about different things, but principally upon our respective countries, more particularly about the United States; in regard to such subjects, Ortiguilla appears to be greatly interested.

I now began to think it time to depart, and consequently signalled for Pete to lead the mule in,—over the beautiful carpet. But if I had no scruples about having it walked on by her, she had, and would not come in. Pete coaxed, muley was obstinate, and though he alternately pulled, pushed, and whipped, not a step would her ladyship take. At last he took my motioned hints, and unloaded her, bringing the articles up himself. These the Inca accepted, and, after examining them attentively, had them removed from the throne room. In a few moments, a train of attendants came in bearing a return of presents of the most magnificent description, one of which I will take space to describe. It is the representation of a bird, the body of which is composed of the most beautiful green feathers, the breast being variegated like that of a humming bird; the wings are of purplish black, and the long tail, of brilliant scarlet. The beak, legs, and claws, are of gold, partially enamelled, and the eyes, are of two rubies, each set round with small brilliants.* It is about two feet high, including the pedestal on which it stands.

Having understood from Onalpo, that the reception of presents was the signal of departure, we took our leave, and returned *home.*

Dinner over, Ned proposed taking a ramble over the city to see what we could see; so he and

* This,—and many other valuable presents, received at various times,—is still in my possession, and together with all the others given to Ned and me during our stay in the valley, form a collection, exceedingly rare and curious. If any of my readers should ever pass through Orangeburg Co., S. C., near the town of that name, they will find, easily, my country box, where it will be shown to the visitor with pleasure.

I got our hats and set off, without a guide, first for the Tianguez, that being the only place with whose situation we were familiar. It is almost a mile and a half from the palace, and we got there much sooner than we expected. There were but a few stalls occupied, and fewer people in the market place. We saw, peeping over the houses at the eastern end, two pyramidal structures, each crowned with a building, and we bent our steps that way to take a closer view. Leaving the Tianguez by a thoroughfare called the Street of the Sun, we passed one block of houses, and, crossing a street, were walking on, when we came against a bronze railing and gate, being part of the enclosure of a large park, in which stood the two edifices mentioned above, and also three or four, long, low, marble buildings on the ground.

Finding we could not obtain an entrance, we turned to our left, in the street we had just crossed, and proceeded along it for several blocks, the park still continuing on our right hand. After passing three streets we came to the north west corner of the enclosure, and turning toward the east we walked one block, when we saw, a short distance before us, that the street was obstructed by a continuation of the park, so we went into the next one on our left, which was narrow and nearly destitute of people.

We loitered along this for five or six blocks, when we became aware of a hum, as of many voices. Hurrying on, a turn in the very crooked street, displayed to our view, a wide thoroughfare —crossing that in which we were,—jammed with men popping in and out of the lower stories of the tall buildings which were erected close together all along both sides of the way. We forced ourselves through the throng to one side, and saw that these lower stories were nothing more nor less than stores, filled with all sorts of beautiful things;—armour, gold and silver services, vases, tripods, articles of clothing, jewelry, furniture, &c. &c. &c. Carried irresistibly, towards the east, we tried, ineffectually, to force ourselves into one of the cross streets. We then inquired of one of the surrounding crowd, what was the name of the thoroughfare in which we were, and were told that it was the Street of the Factories.

Not long after, we crossed a broad way, also crammed with people, and this current overpowering the other, swallowed us up, and we were carried toward the north. We soon learnt that this was the other great commercial street,—that of the Colucatltepec. In a few moments I saw, not far before us, a cubical monument, about sixteen feet high, seven feet square at the base, and four at the top, of white marble, surmounted by a large silver urn, and, as we approached, the crowd divided on each side of it, so as to pass on.

We, however, stopped and perceived that the marble was covered with a hieroglyphical inscription. Happening to glance toward my left, I saw a wide street, meeting that in which we were, at an acute angle, and pointing it out to Ned,—for the noise was so great that it was useless to speak, —we darted through the crowd. We walked on pretty fast for three blocks, and again came in contact with the Street of the Factories, through the moving multitude in which, we penetrated with a great deal of difficulty, and in course of time reached the Tianguez, by the broad streets around which we escaped from the palace.

In the Market Place we were informed that tomorrow will be a market day, and we consequently came home as fast as we could, to commence getting ready to move our merchandize to our stall, which I do not think that I shall like at all. I have a good mind to apply to the Inca for one of the shops in the Street of the Factories, and if I were to do so, I am pretty sure of being successful.

Is it not singular that since I have crossed the

Sierra, I have not laid my eyes upon one of the gentler sex, who do not appear to stir out of their houses. Small children, also, are absolute curiosities. What a comfort!

CHAPTER XII.

The Tianguez.—Visit from the Inca.—A proposed Change of Quarters.—A Walk to see the Premises.—A Remove.

WEDNESDAY, October 13th.—With the rise of this morning's sun we left the palace for the Tianguez with fifteen laden mules, and our stall was soon open. Our stock in trade to-day consisted of agricultural implements, spades, rakes, hoes, shovels, &c., not omitting our two small portable ploughs, harrows and cultivators. These last six articles were conspicuously displayed, and attracted a good deal of attention.

Three hours had passed, and we had had no business, when the Inca suddenly popped in from the back part of the stall and joined us. He examined every thing and appeared much interested in my explanations of the use of the articles. When I had finished my account of the utility of the plough, he said,—"I must see this done, xitulo, (*stranger*). I will come to you before our Master (*the sun*) goes to rest the second time, and we will go out of the walls and see what this thing does."

Soon after he asked if we had seen much of the city as yet, so I told him of our yesterday afternoon's walk, at the same time, hinting that I should prefer a stall in one of the commercial streets, to that which we had in the Tianguez. Orteguilla took the hint readily, and promised to let us have one, but not in either of the streets which we had visited, as they were never honoured with the presence of the lords or ladies of Geral. That which he is going to appropriate to us, is in a third street, which he called—"my street of stores, the Street of the Ocelot." We have to leave the palace while we have a shop, as it is necessary to have a guard over the goods; to this we do not object, and told him that we would visit the street first, and then inform him how we liked it. He remained with us for some time, and then took his leave, but we stayed at our post until half-past two, when we packed up and departed, just as rich in merchandize and poor in pocket as we came, not having sold a single article.

At four Ned and I set out to look for the 'fashionable shopping street of Geral,' under the guidance of a native servant attached to the palace. We left the park by the southern entrance, and walked along the walls as far as the south-eastern corner of the enclosure, when we turned to the right into the thoroughfare which passes in front of the palace, and which is called the Street of the Huaxtepec. Along this we walked, passing two streets;—the third was that of the Ocelot.

This had a row of trees on each side, and the buildings were of all shapes and sizes, standing in large gardens and overshadowed by palm and other trees. There was not a foot passenger to be seen, beside ourselves, in the whole street, if we except the carriers of the numerous splendid litters, some of which were open, but the greater part closed with gilt lattice work. The former were occupied by the curaças and nobles of the Incalate in full feather, while our guide told us that the others were those of the feminine part of the upper classes, but we could not see the occupants, as they did not alight to visit the shops, but were carried, litters and all, into a hall before each establishment.

We went down this street, in admiration of the beautiful shops, and, at length, entered the park surrounding the Inca's palace. We were immediately conducted to him, and he appears to be pleased at our liking 'his Street of Stores,' as he invariably calls it, and promises to have a shop ready for us by the day after to-morrow. We remained some time, and as we left he begged us to visit him frequently in this off-hand manner. The more I see of him, the better I like him, as he appears to be a very sensible, indeed, an intellectual man, and to have a very sound judgment. I do not doubt but that he is one of the best scholars in his little empire.

On arriving at the palace we found a present from Conatzin,—one of the chiefs who conducted us on our arrival in the city,—in the shape of a double palanquin, made of rosewood, lined with scarlet, and having two long handles at each extremity.

Thursday evening, October 14th.—We spent a good deal of the morning in practising two of the horses in a plough, and after some trouble got them in presentably decent kelter. About three o'clock a train of litters made its appearance before the principal entrance, containing the Inca, Cioaco, Movoga Curaça of Poanago, Opanilla, the Lord of the plains, and many dignitaries, with fine faces and long names.

A litter had been provided for Ned and another for me, so that we had not an oportunity of using Conatzin's gift. We got in, the servants mounted their horses, leading two mules loaded with the implements to be tried, and the two horses who were to pull these, followed Peter and John, because they had to, being fastened by ropes to the tails of the animals ridden by those two men. The cortège started. Ascending the terraces of the Huaxtepec, and leaving the city by a small gate, it issued forth upon the great plateau, before the walls, which was to be the scene of our operations.

The parts of the implements were taken off the mules, put together, horses attached, and several furrows made with the plough, much to the satisfaction, of the Inca and his suite, who had descended from their litters, in order to watch the proceedings more narrowly. With equal success but not with equal advantages, the other machines were tried, and the result of the expedition, exhibition, and experiments, was that Orteguilla determined to introduce all of them, on his own lands, to be drawn by llamas; —and, what was of much more consequence to us, he purchased the six on the spot. Having packed up, we returned to the city, so tired that I can scarcely write, and will say no more, save that of all uncomfortable conveniences for transportation, give me an old stage on a rutty road, rather than a litter.

The day subsequent to our agricultural trip, we received word from Apixtamatl, the Lord of Huax, and also the Inca's secretary,—if I may use that word,—that 'the stall of eight sides,' in the Street of the Ocelot, was ready for our reception. So we instantly prepared for a remove to the establishment indicated. The merchandize was put on the mules, the horses were saddled, and away we went guided by the attendant who brought the message.

In twenty minutes we entered a large garden, ornamented with several small fountains, beds of flowers, and groups of trees. In the middle of the front of this garden was a good-sized, octagon-shaped, building of white marble, open in front, the roof being supported by six oriental-like columns. Passing between these we entered a hall, in the shape of a trapezoid, paved with marble. Opposite to the entrance were four more pillars, like the others, permitting a view of the room in the heart of the erection. On either side of the hall was an aperture fitted with a strong bronze gate, partially concealed, as were the whole of the walls, by hangings of pale pink embroidered in silver. The ceiling was of polished rosewood, and though there was no skylight there was a fountain. Leaving this hall we entered the central apartment which was octagon in form, having a diameter of over forty feet. The roof, which was much more elevated than that of the hall, was composed of cedar, richly carved, and ascended on a slight angle to meet the skylight,—by which the room was lit,—under which sparkled a fountain in a porphyry basin. There were no columns except the four leading into the hall, and the floor was composed of different coloured marbles. The tâpestry on the walls was of a bright mazarine blue, embroidered with silver, and curtains of the same, concealed the entrances to the room, which were three in number, without counting that of the hall. About the room were scattered a great many large tables, and seats of all kinds,—it was the '*stall!*'

Reëntering the hall, and passing through the opening on the right, we found ourselves on the threshold of a saloon, of precisely the same size and shape as the hall; and a second succeeded, similar to the first, save that it communicated with the shop. After this second saloon came my chamber. The aperture on the left hand side of the hall, led first into Ned's room, and then into two more, appropriated to the three servants. These six rooms were all lit by small skylights and had fountains. The eighth room corresponded to the hall and was used as a dining room, and a door, or opening in it, opposite the entrance from the shop, communicated with the culinary department, and lodgings of the native servants, who were as numerous here, —in proportion—as in the palace.

I hope that this will give a distinct idea of our temporary habitation, in which, immediately upon our arrival, we began to arrange our goods for the next day's business.

CHAPTER XIII.

The 'Stall.'—Inca's Visit.—The Incaress.*—Moderate Prices.—Business.—Sunday.

On Saturday morning, at nine o'clock, we opened our front gates, and those leading into the shop, seating ourselves, in the latter, to wait patiently for customers, surrounded by velvets, silks, brocades, laces, muslins, shawls, and some rather-out-of-place rugs. Beside these, on a very large table, were displayed two magnificient Persian carpets,—which I mentioned in chapter third,—while four more were spread on the floor. It will be remembered that all these articles had been confided to our care for a trade with Lima or Quito, in which cities foreign goods sell like lightning from their superiority over the native manufactures, and also from their scarcity.

We had not been open five minutes when a litter was carried into the hall and Orteguilla descended from it. I went forward to meet him, but he

*  This most untranslatable word I have rendered above in the best way I could, although in the text I shall use *Empress*, as more pronounceable.

hardly said a word as he gazed fixedly upon the articles displayed in the shop. "How is this?" he asked; "two Suns ago I saw your goods. They were all sharp and turned up the ground. I see them now. They are fit for clothes. How is this?" We explained to him that we had brought many different kinds of things, and that those he now saw were intended, in most cases, for the use of the other sex. He examined everything, and purchased a Persian carpet with which he was in ecstacies, going away soon in order to bring his wife to us.

He had not been gone three-quarters of an hour, when seven or eight closed litters were brought into the hall, guarded by a file of chieftains in full costume. The palanquins were opened, and each permitted the egress of two ladies, who ranged themselves against the walls of the hall, as a golden litter, also guarded, made its appearance on the threshold. This was unclosed and the Inca first came out, followed by a tall and elegant looking female, magnificently attired, who came into the store with him, attended by all the ladies, the chieftains letting fall the curtains between the hall and shop, and guarding all the doors.

"Ahtelaqua, my wife," introduced Orteguilla, addressing Ned and I, who had advanced to meet them,—"I have come to show her your stall." We saluted, and conducted *madame* to a seat, and, while she gazed around at the new goods presented for her inspection, I took a good look at her and her dress. Her long brown hair curled in heavy ringlets over her back and shoulders, being confined around her brow by a golden circlet set with precious stones, having in front, an upright ornament of serpents twisted around a ruby of immense size, from the back of which rose a plume of white feathers. Her complexion was a rich olive, her teeth like pearls, her eyes large and expressive, her nose slightly aquiline, and her forehead, high and intellectual looking. Close around her throat was a gorget of blue cotton cloth, richly embroidered with jewels and silver, and from this depended a long robe of white,—also embroidered,—confined above her waist by a low cut bodice of blue and silver. The skirt was very full, and of sufficient length to form a train, which made her look taller than she really was. Her arms were exposed from the shoulder, where were fastened long, open sleeves of blue, stiff with gems and embroidery. Her small hands and wrists were a mass of the most valuable jewels. Such was Ahtelaqua, and her admiration of our stock was unbounded, which undoubtedly showed her superior judgment. The other ladies, who were scattered over the room, in groups of two or three, sitting and standing without much regard to etiquette,—were habited in a similar manner but with less magnificence, none of them, however, had the right,—as I afterwards found,—to wear more than two feathers in their circlet, while their mistress could carry as *many* as she liked, though not *less* than four.

The empress nearly made our fortunes by the multiplicity of her purchases, although she took but one of the Persian carpets, being evidently frightened at the tremendous price Grey set upon them,—two thousand gold ochols, very near $7,500!) which when Ned mentioned, I turned completely round to see how he had the face to ask so much; but he understood the business, and afterwards told me, that he charged so highly, to afford others a chance of getting one, as he saw glances of admiration pass between the attendant ladies. He was right, as before one o'clock that day, the other four had been sold to the ladies of the suite at a still more extravagant price; and in this manner Ned managed with everything that Ahtelaqua procured. It was a true Yankee trick, but all is fair in trade as well as in war.

As the royal party was beginning to show signs of an intention to leave, Grey ordered Harry Boyd to bring in some prepared tea, that Orteguilla might pronounce his opinion upon that popular beverage. It soon came in two goblets, one of which I gave to the Inca, while Ned presented the other to his Empress. They approved highly of it, so much so indeed that I thought it advisable to give Orteguilla several pounds with full directions how to make use of it, while Grey propitiated the future good will of the Imperial Spouse by the presentation of one of our six beautiful lace veils, and soon after, the whole party departed.

The rest of the morning we were run down with customers, for the Inca had been seen entering, and in the afternoon our stock was nearly cleared out. It was very evident to us that our visit to the valley would turn out a profitable affair not only to ourselves, but to our consignors also.

At seven o'clock we illuminated the shop with hanging lamps and groups of sterine candles, and again it was crowded to suffocation. Our three servants were called in, and all were actively employed until midnight, when we cleared the shop, closed the gates, and retired to rest, a good deal fatigued.

The next day being Sunday, we kept our store closed, much to the astonishment of our heathen visitors, who were rather provoked, that we would not sell anything. We spent all the day in the house, reading and receiving visits in the morning, while the afternoon, and part of the evening were employed by us in arranging our stock for the approaching business of Monday. The remainder of the evening was occupied in walking in our large garden, where I, at last thought of the north and my fireside, for we had no need of a fire or anything like one, the heat being very great without.

CHAPTER XIV.

Selling Out.—The Chronology of Geral.—Another Remove.

On Monday the 18th of October, our establishment contained a rather singular collection of goods to be seen together. On one side were the remnants of Saturday's dealings; on another, cutlery of all kinds; on a third were tea and sugar boxes; on a fourth, cooking utensils; on a fifth, agricultural hardware, and so on around the room.

Nevertheless, we were as busy as before, because we happened to be,—for the time,—'the fashion.' Orteguilla came early and cleared out all our hardware at an immense expense; the ladies of the city entirely swept off Saturday's leavings, the tea, sugar and cooking utensils, of which last I was certain, at the time, that they did not know the use, and I was not astonished in the least degree, when—some weeks after,—while visiting a palace on the Manitepec, I saw a brightly polished, copper tea kettle,—standing on a table in a splendid salon,—filled with flowers!

It was very evident that another day would

close us, and such was the case, as on Tuesday, we were obliged to shut up before noon.

Tuesday evening, October 19th. * * * * *. So after dinner Ned and I sauntered down to the Royal Palace, and, on being announced, were instantly admitted to the Inca, whom we told that we were sold out, merely awaiting his pleasure, to go back to the old palace, as we were residing in a situation which, if immediately taken possession of by another merchant, would prove profitable. Orteguilla then said that our old quarters were at our service for any length of time, upon which I informed him that we intended to leave in the beginning of next *January* saying the word,—without thinking,—in English.

"Jan'ry!" exclaimed the Inca; "what is that?"

"It is the first month of the year," I answered, and here ensued a chronological conversation, which, if I wished, I could not give word for word, and shall therefore take the liberty of putting down what I learnt by it.

The year of these people is divided into fifteen months of twenty-four days each, and these months are subdivided into four weeks of equal length; on every sixth day a market is held. The names of the months are as follows; Olab,—commencing on the tenth of June,—Canno, Malan,

Cop, Koo, Zina, Naon, Pavan, Queloo, Zapx, Kamem, Geb, Allac, Memib, Caxc,—the days composing the first week of every month are called En, Chi-en, Mal-en, Hun-en, Oll-en, Kab-en; those of the second week, Ac, Chi-ac, Mal-ac, Hun-ac, Oll-ac, Kab-ac; those of the third week, Cum, Chi-cum, Mal-cum, Hun-cum, Oll-cum, Kab-cum; and those of the fourth week, Ila, Chi-ila, Mal-ila, Hun-ila, Oll-ila, and Kab-ila. In speaking of a day, its name is placed after that of the month, as Caxc-Kab-ila, which is the last day of the year.

As the number of days, given by the above arrangement, was found to fall five short of the usual and proper number of three hundred and sixty-five, these five are added, regularly, between the end of the month Caxc and the beginning of Olab, consisting of the fifth, sixth, seventh, eighth, and ninth of June. They do not belong to any month, and are named Odar, Nordo, Caman, Sonn, and Tuled.

Not understanding the theory of the Bissextile intercalation of a day, they use a much more exact, but less convenient method, in the end, which, singularly enough, is precisely like that made use of by the inhabitants of Yucatan on the discovery of that peninsula by the Spaniards. How this happened I will not attempt to explain, for the best reason in the world, I do not know myself, and am, therefore, unable to do as I would be done by. They divide *time* into periods of fifty-two of their years, at the end of each of which they intercalate twelve and a half days,—in my opinion, a very inconvenient piece of business. These cycles are called by them, 'sheaves of years,' and are represented by four bundles of thirteen rods each, which are placed in the Council house, and from which the reigning Inca takes one every Caxc-Kab-ila.

In order to designate every year of the cycle with exactness, they divide the latter into four equal parts, representing each fourth by an arrow-head, which is placed in four different positions to denote the separate periods of thirteen years. Dots, from one to thirteen, inclusive, were placed in regular succession before the years of each part, and the four arrow-heads were also repeated with them in order.*

* I feel convinced, on copying the above from my journal, that I have not described this clearly, and therefore give the following table of one cycle, to explain my meaning. It will be seen that by the adjoining simple and ingenious arrangement, the same hieroglyphic never appears twice with the same number of dots, so that any year in the cycle may, at once, be recognized.

First Part.			Second Part.		
Years of Cycle.	Dots.	Hiero-glyphic.	Years of Cycle.	Dots.	Hiero-glyphic.
1	.	↓	1	.	←
2	..	←	2	..	↑
3	...	↑	3	...	→
4	....	→	4	....	↓
5	.....	↓	5	.....	←
6	..... .	←	6	..... .	↑
7	....	↑	7	....	→
8	....	→	8	....	↓
9	....	↓	9	....	←
10	....	←	10	....	↑
11	....	↑	11	....	→
12	....	→	12	....	↓
13	....	↓	13	....	←

Third Part.			Fourth Part.		
Years of Cycle.	Dots.	Hiero-glyphic.	Years of Cycle.	Dots.	Hiero-glyphic.
1	·	↑	1	·	→
2	··	→	2	··	↓
3	···	↓	3	···	←
4	····	←	4	····	↑
5	·····	↑	5	·····	→
6	····· ·	→	6	····· ·	↓
7	····· ··	↓	7	····· ··	←
8	····· ···	←	8	····· ···	↑
9	····· ····	↑	9	····· ····	→
10	····· ·····	→	10	····· ·····	↓
11	····· ····· ·	↓	11	····· ····· ·	←
12	····· ····· ··	←	12	····· ····· ··	↑
13	····· ····· ···	↑	13	····· ····· ···	→

They count their first sheaf from June 10th 1535, when they first settled in the valley: the years,—according to the *civilized* reckoning,—in which their cycles have commenced since that period, are shown in the following table.

Cycles.	Number of Years.	Date.
1		1535
2	52	1587
3	104	1639
4	156	1691
5	208	1743
6	260	1795
7	312	1847

The present year (1847), is the first of the eighth cycle and is thus hieroglyphically expressed.

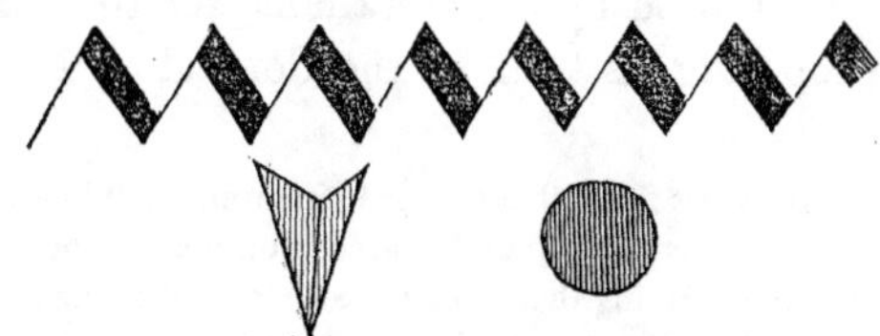

The points indicate the cycle. It will be noticed that seven of them are perfect, while the eighth has but just commenced.

The people believe that in the twelve and a half intercalated days of *some* cycle, the world will be destroyed, and are prone to break everything they can lay their hands on, thinking it useless to keep anything whole, as it can be of no further use to them, if the sun burns them up with the earth.*

The 'Days of Misery,'—as these nearly-baker's-dozen of calamitous supplementaries are called,—having occurred this June, the calendar of Geral is even with ours, for the time, and there will be no more breakage for fifty-two years, but the scenes then enacted have so distressed Orteguilla, that he is determined to avoid them in future, by a new arrangement of the almanac,—if he can find one,—and asked us if we knew of any method by which they could be eluded. We, of course, mentioned our own, and he has requested us to arrange it with names from those of the months and days, used by the Geralians, for the purpose of proposing its trial to the Council of Nobles.†

* I have since found that the manufacturers, stall-keepers, and labourers, merely shut up their places of business without breaking anything, leaving that to be done by the rest of the populace, who would be obliged to replace their domestic articles. It is a singular fact.

† This institution is the only one I met with in the valley, where the Lords and Curaças have the right of debating the sub-

He has ordered Apixtamatl,—his secretary,—to attend on us, so as to be able to inscribe our almanac in hieroglyphics from our dictation, as Ned and I are sadly deficient in that sort of writing.

We took our leave at six o'clock, and returned to the shop, where we packed up our baggage as quickly as we could, and came back to our old quarters in the palace which actually feels like home.

jects brought under their notice, the Inca being absolute in every other matter. The cases which are permitted to be carried before them are limited to a very few.

CHAPTER XV.

The New Calendar.—A visit to an Useful Institution.—
A Present.

FRIDAY, October 22nd,—I have not had time to spare to journalise since Tuesday, on account of our task of arranging the months, weeks, and days, which has occupied every moment. On Wednesday we made out an ephemeris precisely like ours, thirty one days in some months, and thirty in others. This we dictated to Apixtamatl, who appeared to meditate upon every one of the words, so slowly did he make his hieroglyphics. However he finished, at last, about half past four in the afternoon, and immediately carried his laborious production to Orteguilla while we went to our apartment for the purpose of dressing ourselves, in order to take a walk.

Just as we were putting on our hats in the hall, the Inca and his secretary made their appearance, the former bearing in his hand the abominable almanac. Ned dashed his palm-leaf on the table with an audible wish that Orteguilla, Apixtamatl and the calendar, were in a considerably warmer place than a heated Dutch oven, but, notwithstanding, he followed all three into a saloon. Here the Inca made his objections to our method:—there much was too great a difference in regard to the length of the twelve months. We explained the reasons of it, but that would not do; he wanted some arrangement by which the duration of all should be the same. We told him that what he had in his hand was precisely similar to the length of all the months in every civilized country. Nothing would do, and so, after supping with us, —staying until after ten,—and begging us to try some other way, he took his departure.

We went to work again, and all day yesterday were employed in ineffectual attempts to find a suitable plan. It was not until late in the evening that we fixed upon one, which was, this morning, dictated to our poking amanuensis, who conveyed it to the Royal Palace at noon. Orteguilla has expressed his satisfaction with it, notwithstanding the unavoidable extra length of one month, and has announced his intention of placing it before the Council as soon as possible, which he has since told us, will be on Trina-Cum,—next Tuesday.

An hour since we again essayed a sally, but were once more frustrated in our attempt by another visit from the Inca, who came to invite us to accompany him, to-morrow morning, to his mint,*there to have the pleasure of seeing him receive his income, or a portion of it. We accepted, of course, as we have a natural desire to see all that is to be seen. It is now half past six, and not twenty minutes since the Inca left. Here comes Ned to take a walk with me.

Saturday, October 23d. At ten o'clock this morning, Ned and I mounted our horses and galloped to the Royal Palace, where we found Orteguilla waiting for us, seated in his litter and surrounded by all the high officers of the household and the city.

After a slow progress of two miles in an hour, we stopped before a large building on a low terrace. Dismounting, we accompanied the Inca and his suite into a good-sized hall, from which we entered a room, on the left hand side, about thirty feet by twenty, the floor of which was covered to the depth of nearly a foot and a half with silver ochols. In the next room, bronze ones were to be seen in even greater profusion, and in the third apartment, the gold was thrown upon the floor in immense piles, as if from bushel

* In this, as well as in many other cases of the same sort, I have given, instead of the literal translation of the Geralian word, that which we make use of to designate the same kind of institution, or custom, or whatever it may chance to be, that I wish to mention.

baskets. Passing through a large opening we entered a long hall, communicating with the terrace on one side, and on the other, with a vast interior courtyard, filled with natives busily engaged in stamping out the coins. There must have been over eight hundred of these workmen, and the Inca told me that in some buildings, close to the mint, there were twice as many more, all unceasingly employed for twelve hours every day.

The method of forming the coins is easy enough, the only implements required, being a square cutting stamp of copper, and a heavy mallet. The first is placed upon the sheet of metal, in a proper position, and one stroke of the latter suffices to make an ochol.

Orteguilla took his seat upon a dais, and two stools were provided for Grey and me. Here we sat for five hours, 'like Patience on a monument,—smiling in grief,'—and hunger, watching the money being counted into scarlet sacks, by the many officers attached to the institution, and hearing the report of the latter, read by our excellent Apixtamatl, who drawled it over, as he had poked over our calendar, totally unconscious that the two strangers were wishing him at the bottom of the Lake of Naloma, or of the report. At last he did come to an end, and then the scarlet bags were brought in, and placed on the backs of the Indian carriers, who started off on a kind of trot to deposit the money in the magazines, which are in the different island fortresses and fortified palaces. Each sack contains eighteen thousand ochols, and every one of the workmen carried two sacks.

This immense sum is received by the Inca, once in twenty-four days, one-third of it is, however, appropriated to the Sun,* and another third for the payment of salaries, the remainder being solely his, to do with as he pleases. At four o'clock a splendid collation was served, and after we had partaken of it, we returned to the Palace heartily tired. On our arrival at this last place, we found, in each of our chambers, a sack of gold ochols as a present from Orteguilla, which we accepted in the light of a remuneration for having suffered by the tiresomeness of the ceremony. If he sent it with this intention, there is no doubt about his being a sensible man.

While at the mint, Orteguilla conversed with

* This money is expended for the sustenance of the Priests and Vestals of the Sun, and for the support of the poorer Temples. In the same way, as mentioned in the text, the valley,—and the conquered territories, when they have any,—is divided into three parts, and the Sun lands are cultivated for the benefit of the officiators in the Temples.

us for some time, and, among other things, mentioned a singular institution,—having branches in every city of the valley,—called the Tribunal of Music. He has explained to us that it is a committee, having the censorship of all the hieroglyphical literature, the manufactures, &c., and which has a building, where are placed all the articles intended for their inspection. He has promised to take us there as soon as possible, and I do not doubt but that it is well worth seeing.

CHAPTER XVI.

The Council House.—Tribunal of Music.

EARLY on Tuesday morning (October 26th) we were ready and waiting for the Inca's arrival, and at about half past seven we heard an unmistakable evidence of his approach—his band of *music* (?) We hurried to the gate and joined the long procession as it swept past the Palace. It went up the street of the Huaxtepec, and in a short time stopped before a square park, almost entirely occupied by an immense circular structure of white marble and porphyry,—the description of which I will extract from my journal.

'The shape of the building is defined by a double row of vase-like, porphyry columns, supporting a stone roof, entirely detached from the main building, being at a distance of twenty feet from it. The edifice itself is likewise circular, and is surrounded by two piazzas, one above the other, the uppermost being accessible by four broad flights of steps. The lower story is entered by four large openings. The interior of the erection is one vast circular room, open to the sky, and has,—at a distance of fifteen feet from the floor,—a gallery projecting more than twice that distance, and supported by a row of columns similar to those on the exterior of the structure, except that the inner ones are overlaid with silver. Towards the east, the gallery is reached by a wide flight of marble steps, at the top of which is placed the Inca's throne, while the council of Nobles is seated at the foot of the stairs, and facing them. The gallery was filled with ladies in their magnificent dresses, and that part of the floor, which was unoccupied by the numerous Lords and Curaças, was thronged with military officers in their gorgeous costumes.'

Seats were provided for us two by the side of the Inca, and the first subject discussed by the council was our calendar. Many were against change for very excellent reasons, but more were for a better arrangement of the almanac, and the latter carried the day, after a conversation, for they separately said so little at a time, that it could hardly be called a debate. This was gratifying after all our trouble, and it was with real pleasure that we heard the Inca declare that the change should take place on Naon-Ollac, (November 5th,) when the calendar should be placed in the great Temple of the Sun. Seeing that the council was about to take up another subject, in which we could have no interest, Ned and I made our escape, and returned to the Palace.

Several days now passed without anything particular occurring, as we did nothing but go shopping in the three business streets and pay visits to our numerous acquaintances, sometimes to Orteguilla, who occasionally returned them,—or, at least, came to do so,—for we were generally out.

Monday, November 1st. At six o'clock this morning,—just as we rose from our breakfast table,—Orteguilla arrived with a few attendants, to escort us to the Tribunal of Music. We instantly put on our hats, ordered Conatzin's present to be brought to the gate of the Park, got into it, and set out. Our beautiful palanquin is very comfortable, the double weight preventing the uneasy motion of the single litter. In about half an hour we got to our destination, which is a square building, one story high, and surrounded by an immense flower garden, beautifully laid out, and containing a few fountains. The edifice is constructed of a buffish coloured stone, richly carved, with a false second story, pierced with lattice work of the most elaborate description.

We entered by a handsome portal, decorated with the most delicate carving, and found ourselves in a large room, serving as a vestibule, where the Inca was received by the officers of the institution, who are appointed by him, and who receive large salaries by law. We left this vestibule by a door on the right, entering the business apartment of the Tribunal, where we saw about fifteen natives, squatted on the floor, busily engaged in recording the transactions of the officers, in hieroglyphics, which are formed with four colours, red, blue, yellow and green placed,—in a liquid state,—in porcupine quills, used something in the same way as we use pens.

Leaving this office,—which forms the south-western corner of the building,—we entered a very long room lit by large skylights and lattice work, and having a continued, broad shelf running round the walls, at a height of four feet from the floor. On this were placed hundreds and hundreds of manuscript hieroglyphical books, in various forms, some being rolled up like the ancient papyri, while the greater portion were folded up in the manner of the Chinese and Japanese books, with a board at each end. At equal distances around the apartment were the readers of the Tribunal, seated on comfortably cushioned stools. All these works have to be read, their worth reported to the principal officers, and a stamp affixed to them, previous to their being permitted to be multiplied and distributed for sale.* The whole of this is done without expense to the author, who has only to send a copy of his work to the library of the Inca, which must in consequence, be of great size, and which we have been invited to visit whenever we wish.

Besides all this trouble taken by the tribunal, prizes are given to the writers of the best, and by these means,—Orteguilla tells me,—the number of useful works is greatly augmented. Having traversed the Literary department, we went into the room in the northern end of the building, which is by far the largest, and is devoted to manufactures.

This contains six broad tables, running the entire length, beside a very wide shelf around the walls, which last are covered with specimens of different kinds of tapestry, carpets, variously colored cotton cloths, feather-work, furs, striped stuffs, figured materials, and prepared buff coloured skins embroidered with thin pipes of gold and silver, or with stained quills of the Brazilian Porcupine. Other parts of the walls

* I was informed,—a few days after this visit,—that in the City of Geral alone, over 37,000 persons found employment in copying works for the authors, at a very small remuneration, and of these, nearly 32,000 were females!

sustained dresses, armour, and warlike, domestic and agricultural implements, arranged in the manner of trophies. On the shelf were placed tables, stools, ottomans, and other large domestic articles, litters, palanquins, and military as well as civil contrivances, for transportation; also, the larger manufactures of a demi-civilized nation.

On the tables stood gorgeous services of gold and silver splendidly wrought, immense vases of the same metals; tripods, standing censors, incense tables, candelabras, of bronze, or the two above named precious metals, inlaid with mother-of pearl, or jewels; glittering ornaments of different gems, beautifully cut and set; *glass* mirrors, vases, goblets, pitchers, dishes and an uncountable number of other magnificent luxuries. All these articles, are merely sent to the Tribunal for competition, the most splendid of each sort receiving a prize.

On one of the tables I noticed some most exquisitely formed *china** services, vases, &c.,

* The reader is doubtless surprised at finding glass and china among these people, but I solemnly assure him that such is the fact. Pottery was practised by the ancient Peruvians, but whether the art of making glass was used, or even known I am not able to say. There was sufficient time for the Spaniards to have taught them both before Toparca's death.

painted with flowers, birds and figures, in vivid colours, without the slightest resemblance to nature, and drawn in bold defiance of all the rules of perspective. I should have mentioned before, that the mirrors were not silvered, but were backed with black cloth.

We left this room, and passed into the central court, as the remainder of the edifice consists of the private apartments of the officers. In this there were several fountains of different forms, carved out of marble; none of them very handsome. As we re-entered the vestibule, in order to return home, the Inca raised a hanging, on the right-hand side of it, and we saw a small room, lit by a skylight, in which stood a group of figures, as large as life, cut out of a softish kind of stone! We were much surprised at seeing such a large attempt at sculpture in this part of the world, although it was horribly bad, distressingly so, if it had happened to appear in one of our modern galleries. It is intended to represent Orteguilla, Ahtelaqua, their son Onaméva, and their daughters, Ineralla and Garoda; the faces of the first two were certainly like, but not by any means flattered; the originals of the last three we had never seen.

The Inca thinks it perfection, but I have seen many, in the different palace parks, and streets of Geral, intended for fountains, infinitely better;—there were two small figures,—about forty inches high,—meant for a fountain, standing near the large group, and which, in my opinion, ought to have put the latter to the blush, so many times better is the lesser group.* We got to the palace at half-past eleven, having been four hours and more at the institution, and, although I am completely tired out, I would not have missed the visit on any account, as I have not spent a more agreeable morning,—to the best of my recollection,—since we took our departure from the United States.

* These two figures I purchased, not long afterwards, for one hundred and fifty gold ochols, (490 dollars, about), and they now form part of my collection. The name of the sculptor is,—or was,—Coançotzin.

CHAPTER XVII.

An excursion.—The Upper Lake.—Patapalanamit.—Iztinapan.—Pocotatl.—Return to Geral.—Temple of the Sun.

NOT having anything to detain us in town, and the weather being extremely warm, we accepted an invitation from Cioaco, the Curaça of Ocopaltepec,—our oldest acquaintance in the valley,—to make a short trip with him through the environs of the Capital, and started, on Tuesday, November 2nd, at dawn.

The Curaça travelled in a litter, but we preferred our horses, and consequently made use of them, instead of the splendid, uncomfortable, jolting palanquins, which our travelling companion had brought for our use. We were accompanied by our three servants,—the poor mules being left to take care of themselves in the park—and Cioaco had a tribe of his household attendants in his train.

We crossed the city to the foot of the terraces of the Geral-tepec, and ascending them, were, by ten o'clock, on the lowest of the northern plateaus of the Sierra Paricis. Continuing on this, we directed our course towards the south for two hours, until we came to a stream, which we followed for about twenty minutes, when we arrived at the 'Upper Lake' by which the city is supplied with water. At the outlet of this lake into the stream, along which we had been proceeding, there is a waterfall of about eighteen feet, at the foot of which are situated the water-works, extensive stone buildings with water wheels.

We were admitted, and examined them, while a meal was in course of preparation. The machinery is very simple, being composed of several large wheels with buckets attached to their broad edges. The lowest of these throws the water from its buckets,—which are filled by passing through the stream,—into a tank, elevated some distance above the level of the stream. From this tank the element is removed by a second wheel to another tank higher up, and so on until the water reaches the top of the building, where there is a capacious reservoir, from which it is distributed through the city by means of bronze pipes.*

At a little before three we started again, in a

* The learned, or travelled reader will perhaps recognize,—as I did,—in the above described machinery, a by no means slight resemblance to the '*Persian Wheel*,' so much used in Egypt and Nubia.

westerly direction, and soon came to the walls of the City of Geral, which are over eighty miles around, enclosing an area of more than three hundred square miles, of which three-fourths are occupied by a dense population, and the remainder by scattered blocks of habitations. We got outside of the walls by means of a pass from the Inca,—a string from the borla,—which carried us through a finely defended gate,—and at sunset we reached the little, unwalled town of Patapalanamit, situated on the second plateau of the Sierra. Here we spent the night, and started the next morning for the village of Iztinapan, where we breakfasted at the house of Mixtecaltzin, who, it will be remembered, was the chief that conducted us from Quauhtitlan to Geral, on our arrival in the valley.

From this village we had a commanding view of the capital. About ten we took leave of our kind host and set out for Pocotatl, descending the two plateaus, in just as many hours, on a fine causeway.

There was no beautiful scenery, and it was excessively hot, so we wished ourselves in the palace, and that the Curaça had not thought of asking us to accompany him. After a scorching ride, we arrived in the above named town at dusk, retiring to rest immediately, in order to be prepared for the return to the capital on the morrow.

Thursday was even hotter than the day before, and several of the Curaça's followers gave out, being obliged to seek shelter in the numerous houses that lined the way. At six in the evening we reached Onadella, and pushed forward over the dikes as fast as possible, in order to get into Geral before the gates were shut,—we were just in time. We were glad enough, that night, to put ourselves in our large, cool chambers, and I, for one, slept very well, notwithstanding the fatigue consequent upon such a long ride, and my anxiety to see the ceremony at the Temple of the Sun, which was to take place at five in the morning.

Friday, November 5th.—Ned and I arose at four, and after partaking of a light breakfast, proceeded to the Inca's palace as fast as our horses could go, arriving there at dawn, (25 minutes of 5.) The terrace, ante-chambers, audience room, and saloons, were all illuminated, and filled with nobles in their magnificent peace costumes, glittering with gems, for this was an occasion when they were permitted to appear before the Inca without their black robes, and they did ample justice to the permission by dressing as gorgeously as possible.

Orteguilla entered the throne room almost at the same time that we did, and all repaired, at once, to the street. Litters were not allowed, except one for the Inca, and he, seating himself in it gave the signal for departure. Ned and I also walked, leaving our horses on the terrace. After passing a few blocks, we came to the railings and gate, which had prevented our progress on the twelfth of October. The latter was now wide open, and, on passing through it, we saw that we were in an immense park, while not far before us, were two tall, semi-pyramidal structures, each supporting a large terrace, on which was built a temple.

We ascended to the terrace of the most eastern one, by means of a broad flight of steps, the foot of which was guarded by two serpent's heads,—longer than those in front of the Old Palace,—their bodies forming a barricade on each side of the flight. All around the edge of the terrace was a stone wall about twelve feet high, covered with basso relievos, and in the centre of the platform was a second flight of steps leading to a higher terrace, on which was a long building of the purest white marble, with an artificial second story, and a tall tower at each end. In front of this structure the platform was covered with the Priests of the Sun, dressed in trailing draperies of white embroidered with gold suns. Orteguilla was received at the top of the second flight by the High Priest, a fine looking man of about thirty-five or forty years of age, wearing a sky blue robe, without sleeves, richly embroidered around the throat and arm holes with gold points, and on the remaining portion with gold suns. Around his neck hung a large, golden-rayed disc, representing the orb of day.

The procession now entered the Temple by a long hall, filled with priests, which led us into a monstrous apartment, the walls and ceiling being hung with skyblue. A broad cornice of gold encircled the room, and opposite the entrance, hung an enormous convex, circular plate of gold, at least five feet in diameter, having innumerable rays. In front of this, on a long dais covered with white cloth richly embroidered with gold scroll work, stood a large white marble altar, with gold ornaments. On the top of this, and on the front edge, was an oval vase of the same precious metal, of exceedingly graceful form, with two handles of twisted serpents, altogether about eighteen inches in height, and thirty long in the oval. Behind this was placed a cabinet, of gold, three feet high, magnificently chased, with a gate of silver studded with sapphires and topazes, as were the brim and stand of the vase.

Around the altar were fifteen more vases, of large size, representing the months of the year, the name of one month being inscribed upon each vase, all of which are arranged in the order of the months. In these immensely valuable vases,—they are of solid gold,—incense was burnt during the whole ceremony,* and they were surrounded by crowds of vestal virgins clad in robes of blue embroidered with gold suns. The temple was illuminated by perfumed lamps that hung around the altar and cornice, and by many candelabras that were scattered about the floor.

A moment after we entered, the drapery at the eastern end of the sanctuary was drawn up, and the first rays of the rising sun, entering the apartment, paled the before brilliant lamps. The High Priest advanced to the altar, and lit a fire in the vase of sacrifice upon it, taking the flame from the seventh of the surrounding vases.† He then approached Orteguilla, who, after receiving from Apixtamatl the scroll inscribed with the new calendar,‡ presented it to the High Priest.

* The incense consisted of Tonquin and Vanilla beans, and the fumes of these, when burnt, are very unacceptable; enough so to make the Sun turn up his nose, or smell some Cologne.

† That of the month in which we were according to the old style;—Naon.

‡ This calendar I have placed in Appendix Number Two,—

This personage held it over the flame he had lit in the altar vase, and after reading it aloud, with his face toward the rising sun, placed it in the cabinet, with many genuflexions, while the priests and vestals sang away for dear life, each appearing to sing entirely upon his, or her, own hook. The effect may be imagined, but not described. This was the whole of the simple ceremony, so we immediately retreated to the terrace, and commenced picking our way down the steep steps* of the pyramid, at an imminent danger of descending faster than we wished, and of alighting upon our precious nose.

together with the old one,—for the edification of those of my readers who wish to know how time was reckoned in Geral,—for that year, at least.

* Excepting this flight of steps, the sides of the whole supporting structure were even, slippery, steep, and of highly polished granite, being totally inaccessible.

CHAPTER XVIII.

A Visit to the Royal Library.—An Invitation.—The Palace of the Manitepec.—An Incident.

MONDAY, November 15th.—Ten days have been passed by us in wandering over the city without any particular object, and it was not until this morning that Ned bethought him of the invitation we had received from the Inca to visit his library whenever it so pleased us, and we consequently determined to go at once. So at nine o'clock we set out on foot for the Royal Palace, and after walking through the Tianguez to see what was to be seen there, we crossed to the Park and obtained entrance to Orteguilla.

We sat talking with him for some time, and casually mentioned the library, which we were again asked to examine. On acquiescing to his proposal, we followed the Inca out of the palace, to the southwestern corner of the Park, which we left by a handsome bronze gate, and were conducted across the street,—that of the Terraces,—to a large garden in the centre of which stands a building of white marble, richly carved,—the library. Entering the structure by a fine, wide portal, we found ourselves in a hall, hung with mazarine blue tapestry; passing through this vestibule, we stood in a large apartment nearly filled with tables which were piled up with manuscripts of all shapes and sizes.

Orteguilla tells us that there are eighteen sacks of books,* but I think that hardly possible. We poked about among the tables for at least two hours, exercising ourselves in the art of hieroglyphics, and then,—taking leave of the Inca,—went to the street of the Ocelot, where we hunted up a book stall, entering and depriving the same,—at an unwarrantable expense,—of divers curious and, no doubt, interesting manuscripts, of which we could scarcely make out the titles. Having commenced, we continued shopping until nearly one o'clock, when we returned to *our* Palace.

I neglected to mention that, while we were in the library, we received an invitation from Orteguilla to spend some days with him at his country Palace on the Manitepec, where he intends to go on Thursday,—the eighteenth inst.,—and the

* A sack holds, or is supposed to hold, eight thousand, it being a hieroglyphic expressing that number. This would make the library count one hundred and forty-four thousand volumes, which is, in my opinion, about twice too much. I doubt if it counts the forty-four thousand, letting alone the hundred thousand.

weather being so very oppressive,* that in spite of the uninterestingness of our late excursion with the Curaça of Ocopaltepec,—we accepted without the slightest hesitation.

The next two days were spent in preparing for our visit to the country, and we found that we should be obliged to leave two of our servants in the city to take care of the mules, as the natives were too much afraid of them to attend to them well. We left all our superfluous baggage in the Palace, and were accompanied by Harry Boyd, who was to take charge of the two baggage mules that formed our train,—or rather to cook our meals, as we had not lived long enough in Geral to be accustomed to do without tea or coffee, which last,—although it grows wild on the northern side of the hills,—they do not cultivate or make use of,—we did, often, and found it of superior quality.

Thus divided, we started, on Thursday morning at daybreak, for the Inca's city Palace, where we joined his cortège, which was not very large, as his family had preceded him by three or four days, carrying the greater part of the court in their train.

* I have placed,—in Appendix Number Three,—the state of the thermometer, as I noticed it during my stay in the valley.

The procession of palanquins,—we used Conatzin's present, to which we had contrived to fasten two riding horses, one before and the other behind, harnessed between the poles,—left the terrace at six o'clock, and traversed the city in an easterly direction, passing by the numerous public parks that ornament that quarter of the capital. We got to the walls at ten, after having gone about nine miles, and here the litter carriers were changed for the third time, since the cortège had started. We now proceeded on slowly, skirting the bases of the mountains.

It was not until four in the afternoon that we came in sight of our destination, and I never saw a more beautiful view. In the triangle formed by the bases of three mountains, terraced nearly to their snow-capped summits, stood a very extensive park, having a high railing of gilt bronze, overshadowed with luxuriant trees, between the bolls of which could be seen the glistening of white marble buildings and silvery fountains. The gates were thrown wide open, and the broad avenue of trees, along which we passed to reach the palace, was lined, on each side, with nobles and their retainers, all in gala costume.

The avenue, I should think, was nearly two miles in length, winding all through the park,

RICHARDSON—COX, N.Y.

varied by beautiful pavilions, and the largest kind of fountains, perfect cataracts of water.

At last, a sudden turn in the wide road displayed to our view the vast edifice to which we were hastening,—a mass of richly carved, and highly polished white marble. Ascending to a semi-circular platform by four shallow *steps*,—they might almost have been called *terraces*, as each was sufficiently broad to admit of a double row of columns, of the usual Geralian form, which supported the projecting roof,—we found ourselves in front of a long and wide hall, supported by eight rows of gold, or gilt, pillars, each row containing,—as we subsequently found,—fifty-two. The beams, that divided the ceiling into squares, were carved and gilt, while the squares themselves, as well as the four walls of the hall, were mirrors. The floor was of white marble, and the immense vestibule was lit by long rows of skylights between every other range of columns.

This hall opened into an enormous circular room, with four concentric rows of porphyry columns to support the mirrored ceiling, in the centre of which was a large, round, skylight. Underneath this last was a grand fountain, which, I suppose, had figures in the centre of it, but they were entirely concealed by the descending torrent of water.

Beyond this splendid rotunda were the suites of rooms intended for our occupation. Tall golden vases ornamented the corners of my chamber; the stools and tables were carved and gilt; so were the pillars supporting the skylight; the tapestry on the walls was so thickly embroidered in gold, with curiously formed animals and scrolls, that the crimson groundwork could only be seen, here and there, in little patches; and my bed and cushions were wrought in an equally lavish style.

All around me was magnificence, but I was satiated with it, and even the positive grandeur of this palace failed to give rise to those feelings, with which I first entered the Old Palace in Geral. Then, everything that I saw was entirely different from, and superior to what I had expected to find, but a month's residence had deprived Splendour of her greatest charm,—Novelty. In the Palace of the Manitepec, however, there did happen to be something that was new to us,—a residence in the midst of all the pomp and gorgeousness of the Inca's Court, and this made two weeks pass away too rapidly, causing us to be quite surprised, on the second of December, at Orteguilla's informing us that he should return to the capital the next day, in order to prepare for his annual tour through the principal cities of the valley, during which journey he wished for our company. Consequently we got ready to depart, and on the third of December left for Geral.

On reviewing the journal of our residence on the Manitepec, I find but one incident worthy of insertion here. The young lady mentioned was about fourteen years of age.

'Tuesday, November 23d. About eight o'clock last evening, I was sitting in one of my four rooms, writing in this journal by the light of a standing lamp, the oil of which, by the way, was perfumed most delightfully with vanilla, when Ned,—who had been walking in the Park with Orteguilla and his family,—rushed in, wringing wet, and told me to follow him, as Ineralla, the Inca's eldest daughter, had fallen into an artificial lake and been nearly drowned, before he (Ned) could rescue her.

'Of course, I went with him immediately, with my medicine chest in my hands, and, after passing through many dark rooms, a tapestry was raised, and we found ourselves on the threshold of the Empress' private saloon,—a large, square apartment, with splendid furniture, and draped walls, brilliantly illuminated by pendent lamps, of which, two or three hung between each of the porphyry columns that supported the skylight. By the side of a beautiful fountain that bubbled in the centre of the room, was placed a large ottoman of crimson starred with gold, and on this lay the insensible and dripping form of Ineralla, her wet, white drapery forming a good contrast with the magnificence of the dresses of her family who surrounded her, together with the numerous attendants, who chafed her hands and unsandalled feet, fanned her, and did all they could to restore consciousness.

'Her head rested on her mother's lap, and her dark hair, curled by the water, fell in heavy volumes on the marble floor. I instantly saw that she was in no imminent peril from her unsolicited bath, but had fainted from fright, and I, consequently exerted all my powers to render her, once more, sensible. My efforts were crowned with success, and by nine o'clock that evening she was in a deep sleep.'

The young princess awoke the next morning with a slight fever, but in two or three days was perfectly restored to health, much to our credit, and we were overwhelmed with thanks and gifts from all her now happy family.

CHAPTER XIX.

Tezcutlipotenango.—Otompan.—Mixocolo.—The Covered Market Place.—Poanango.

On Wednesday morning, December 8th, Ned and I, together with Harry Boyd,—we two in our 'horse litter,' our cook mounted, and followed by four mules, two of which were loaded,—joined the Inca's magnificent escort as it left the city by the Great Dyke. This was an occasion of state, and all the highest officers of the Incalate, the nobles, curaças, and principal chieftains, were obliged to attend in Orteguilla's train, which formed an interminable procession of gorgeous litters and palanquins. The Inca's palanquin was carried by sixteen nobles, and surrounded by a guard of warriors, of which a perfect army, marched before and behind the showy array of nobility.

Passing through the four island fortresses,—which were decorated with flaunting banners, and garlands of flowers,—we regained the shores of the Lake at Onadella, by nine o'clock. At this town Orteguilla visited the bronze foundries, and show rooms, in the last of which, he showed me several ploughshares, excellent imitations of our iron ones, but I doubted whether the material of which they were composed was stout enough, it being copper with an alloy of tin.

At eleven we set out again, after having partaken of a collation prepared for the Inca and his suite, and about four in the afternoon arrived before the walls of Tezcutlipotenango,—(a short name, by the way !)—where we were received by dense crowds of the populace, and by the Curaça of the 'Circular City,'—as it is likewise called from its peculiar form,—who had preceded us from Onadella, he having started with the Inca.

The procession entered the walls and was conducted to the palace, which was situated in the very centre of the city, and was of great size, although without the slightest pretensions to beauty. Leaving Boyd to look out for lodgings in some house or other,—Ned and I started, on a tour of the city, from the Palace Park, immediately opposite the entrance of which was the commencement of a wide street leading to one of the many city gates. Down this we bent our steps, but we had not got to the first cross street, when we saw that our progress was impeded by a strong bronze chain, drawn across the thoroughfare in which we were, and guarded by a good many warriors, fully armed, who would not permit us to pass.

Being, *openly*, unarmed,—though we perpetually carried each a 'Colt's revolver,'—and, taking this into our thoughts, not considering twelve shots sufficient to drive away at least a hundred men, we retreated, on deciding that 'Discretion is the better part of Valour,'—forgetting that, as the guards were nothing but *barbarians*, they would be alarmed at the sound of a single discharge, letting alone the execution that would not fail to be attendant upon such a noise, when either Ned or I fired in anger.* We tried two or three other streets with no better success, and so 'gave it up as a bad job,' returning to the Palace, where we found that apartments had been prepared for us by order of the Inca. The evening was passed by this last named personage, in receiving the officers of the city, and the reports of the different manufactories, which were put away by Apixtamatl, in order that they might be read before the Council of Nobles in the capital, on the return of the Inca.

Thursday, December 9th.—Two months since

* It may not be out of place to remark here, that during our residence in the valley, only one shot was fired, and that will be mentioned in its proper place. (Chapter XX.)

we entered the Valley, and nearly four since we left Charleston! As Orteguilla intends to go through his principal cities as quickly as possible, he left Tezcutlipotenango this morning, early, for Otompan, where we arrived in an hour and a half. This city is much smaller than the other, although the walls enclose a much greater space. The stream of Naloma,—which passes through it as well as through Geral and Tezcutlipotenango,—is crossed by many bridges, of rather stronger construction than the flimsy article over the Arinos at Povoacao, as they well may be.

The Naloma, at this city, is not quite half a mile broad,* and besides a stone pier on each bank, a great many more,—twelve, and even twenty, in some cases, are built in the water, the tops of all being connected by strong beams of wood, on which are laid thick slabs of granite, strongly cemented. A solid stone parapet is erected on each side of these bridges, which are quite low. Both sides of the stream,—in all the cities through which it winds its course,—are built up with polished stone, and are much used as a promenade by the inhabitants.

† By the map of the valley, it is over a mile wide, as I could not make it as small as it really should be, without running the risk of confounding it with the causeways.

Orteguilla took up his station in the palace, and gave an audience to the officers of the city, as he did last night in Tezcutlipotenango. We dined about one o'clock, and set out, immediately after having done so, for the third curaçial city—that of Mixocolo,—where we arrived at half past three. This is larger than either of the two cities through which we have passed, and contains many splendid public buildings, which, however, we could only see from the Park of the Palace, as the Inca is carefully guarded by large bodies of warriors, no one being allowed to enter the Park but the municipal authorities, and no one to leave without a pass from Orteguilla, who, after he had received and dismissed his visitors, came and told us to follow him, as he wanted to show us the principal curiosity of the city.

Issuing from the guarded gates without the slightest difficulty,—our conductor being recognized,—we were led "down one street and up another," until, after threading a perfect labyrinth, we passed before a building, about thirty feet high and a hundred wide, the front being very richly carved out in granite, but without any opening, save a large gateway in the centre. The sides were not visible, being blocked up with houses. Through the gate, crowds of people came out, and as many went in, while Ned and I wondered what the attraction was in the curious looking structure.

The Inca pushed himself into the entering throng, closely followed by us, and the resistless human current carried us in. Before us was spread an apparently interminable vista of vase-like, white marble columns, supporting seven rows of large skylights. Beneath the centre row of these last was the broad passage for the purchasers, for on either side were stalls or shops, divided by low partitions, so that an uninterrupted view could be had from any part of the queer looking edifice. The purchasers' passage was crammed, and presented a gay appearance from the differently coloured dresses of the buyers. We were in the covered market place, and it is over a mile long, entirely constructed of granite and marble. We walked the whole length and returned, purchasing a great many articles. We did not get back to the palace until long after eight, and I have just come to my room, after having partaken of a supper prepared by Harry Boyd, for Ned, me, and himself.

Friday, December 10th. It sprinkled this morning as we started from Mixocolo, being the first specimen of rain that we have experienced since we landed at Para, the dry season having been in full force ever since, and it ought to last from September to February in this elevated region. I hope we shall have no more of it, as I neither fancy remaining in the valley for the six wet months, nor going back to the Atlantic coast in the mud. We left the stream this morning, and have been proceeding in a westerly direction all day, over stone causeways, along which I have noticed large, fortified stone buildings which I found, on inquiry, to be magazines of military stores, built so that whenever the army is obliged to cross through the country, it can do so without injury to the crops of any of the inhabitants, thus avoiding all the desolation, that,—unfortunately,—so often marks the route of even friendly troops in time of war. The army of Geral is very large, I find, in order to repel the constant aggressions of the savage tribes without the valley, who too frequently cross the Sierra, enter the Inca's territory, and often do much mischief.

We dined to-day, at a village, whose name I could not learn, in a large tent, there being no edifice of sufficient size to accommodate the whole of Orteguilla's rather numerous retinue,—and, at dusk, we arrived at this town,—Poanango. It is quite small, and the governor's residence is too circumscribed to include accommodations for us, who are, in consequence, quartered on a private house. However, it is only for to night, as the Inca leaves at daybreak for the city of Xaromba.

CHAPTER XX.

Atalatl.—Xaromba.—A Visit to the Salt Mines.—A Dangerous Piece of Fun.

SATURDAY, December 11th.—We set out at the appointed time, and advanced for six hours, merely stopping about every mile and a quarter, at the Chasquis stations to change the carriers of the litters, which we personally had not to do, on account of our horse palanquin which has proved an exceedingly comfortable sort of conveyance, and attracts much admiration from the nobles. The splendidly carved and polished rosewood body is close to the ground, and the horse in front, is harnessed at a sufficient distance from the palanquin to prevent his kicking the front of it in, as he could easily do, if he were near enough. Fortunately the handles are very long, as the intention was to have it carried by sixteen men, four on each handle.

At a little before noon we arrived in Atalatl, a good-sized town, where we remained during the heat of the day, leaving at four in the afternoon for Xaromba. We were then rapidly approaching the northern boundary of the valley, and the towering, hoary-headed, needle-like, Atolatepec, with all its terraces of many shaded green, is in full view from the window,—if I may so call an opening into which fits a thin slab of white jasper, now turned on one side,*—at which I am sitting, in the Palace of Xaromba. I have written that this immense peak rose directly before me, and I will add that to the north of it, is the Xaromba-*tepec;* I should call it a *hill* by the side of its gigantic neighbour, on whose right, the Valley of Geral stretches its rolling plains toward the south,—a mass of habitations,—almost a single city.

We arrived in this walled town at seven o'clock, and the sun has now been down some time, the scene spread before me, being bathed in the light of the moon, which has been shining so long that the welcoming fires have nearly died out. Here is Grey after me, to go up with him to the roof of the Palace, so good night.

Sunday, December 12th. You have, of course, heard the proverb which runs something like

* This was the first time I had seen anything in the Valley of Geral, at all resembling our casement windows. The opening in the wall was square, and the air could be excluded, while the light was still admitted, by an exceedingly thin slab of the mineral, above mentioned, which is more than *semi*-transparent.

this,—'Do at Rome as Romans do,'—and will, in consequence, pardon me for having gone to the salt mines here with the Inca and his suite, this morning, for as the Geralians have no particular day set aside for religious observances, they did not think it wrong to go.

Starting on foot from the palace at eight o'clock in the morning, we crossed through the beautiful 'City of Fountains,'—as I believe its name implies,—and ascending the Xarombatepec to the second plateau, we stopped to rest ourselves, after a toilsome ascent, in a large tent broadly striped with dark blue. About ten o'clock, the superintendant of the salt mines came and announced that the Inca,—who had been accommodated with a separate tent,—was on his way to the entrance of the works.

We sprang off our couches and hurried to the place indicated,—a large doorway composed of huge blocks of the clearest rock salt. Passing through this we entered a gallery, cut out of the earth, but ceiled, walled, and floored, with square blocks of salt. It was illuminated by candelabras, placed between the graceful, vase-like, columns of salt, that appeared to support the roof. This gallery is very long, and on turning a sudden corner we found that it was continued in the form of an inclined plane, gradually descending towards the eastern, or the same side on which we entered the mountain.

The first gallery,—which, as well as all the others, I measured by paces to the best of my ability,—is about six hundred feet long, and the first inclined plane nearly fifty feet less, at the end of which is a second gallery, seven hundred feet in length, succeeded by a flight of four hundred and twenty-seven steps. All these lead in the same direction as the plane, but a third gallery was excavated towards the centre of the mountain for a distance of eight hundred feet, ending in a vast circular saloon, at least twelve hundred feet in diameter, with a ceiling that I am sure is partly a natural formation, it being very highly vaulted, for to cove a ceiling would be far above the ingenuity of any workmen I have yet met with in the valley. This immense apartment was brilliantly illuminated by hanging lamps, candelabras, and torches, and in the centre of it was a large oblong table of salt, on which was laid a collation that was soon demolished by the Inca and his suite. I was much disappointed with the effect of the lights in this salt apartment, there being a glaring reflection, but none of those exquisite crystals that I noticed in the celebrated mines of Wielicska, near Cracow.

The repast being finished, the hall was emptied

by an egress on the opposite side to that on which we entered. A short entry led us to the top of a winding staircase, which consists of six hundred and nineteen steps, where there is a landing place and two openings admitting the visitor into several ranges of apartments, all illuminated, supported by columns, and nearly un-look-atable, from the horrible yellow reflections of the flickering lamps.

Returning to the staircase we descended thirty-two steps, when a second platform and opening permitted us to enter a second series of apartments, larger than those we had just visited and equally disagreeable. Here the superintendent told us that we were on a level with the valley, which was as much as saying that we had descended over two thousand five hundred feet.

We now went down a series of eight inclined planes, constructed so as to form a zigzag through the mountain, and similar to the galleries, &c., above, that is to say, formed of salt blocks, supported by columns, and illuminated,—and conducting us above five hundred feet downwards in a direct line. Turning into a short entry leading towards the east, we soon entered an excavated room, seventy feet square, with a ceiling ascending to a sharp point.

I now heard a sound like the rushing of a cataract, and Ned also observed it, but we thought nothing of it. We left the saloon by a second entry leading towards the south, one hundred and seventy feet long, and rather darker than the others, or appeared to be so, after the brightness of the room. As we proceeded along it, the noise, which we had observed in the chamber, grew louder and louder, and the cause of it was revealed, when, at the end of the entry, the superintendent raised a very thick piece of tapestry.

Immediately opposite the opening thus revealed, from a semi-circular cavity,—dark as Erebus, and elevated, at least, two hundred feet above the level on which we were standing,—fell a torrent of water, with a roar like thunder, losing itself in an immense ravine, the edges of which were defended by a parapet of large salt blocks! We rushed from the entry, and stood on the polished floor of a vast, natural, salt cavern, of the size and appearance of which nothing from my pen can convey an adequate idea. Illuminated as it was by candelabras on the floor, by torches in profusion as high up as the opening from which the water fell, and by hanging lamps from every projecting crystal within the reach of the climbers,—the enormous hall could not be totally seen, and as for the high vault over our heads, we could only know it to be there by the brilliant reflection of a more elevated light than common, upon a pendent crystallization, which shone like stars far, far up. The natural columns, and the arches which they appeared to support, the vaults and niches to be seen here and there, the *stalactites* and *stalagmites*, were all illuminated, and glittered in unrivalled brilliancy, in every colour of the rainbow.

Close to the cataract, Grey pointed out to me an opening leading to a smaller cave, and in which he had discovered an *exact* representation of a gothic door; the pointed arch was surrounded by a projecting stratum of a purplish coloured salt, forming the ornaments above the portal, and on each side was a buttress, surmounted by a pinnacle. Of course all was uneven in height and dimensions; and, perhaps, I should never have recognized the *exact* resemblance, had not Grey pointed out all the details separately. He commenced making a hasty sketch of it, including the cataract, while I passed through the gothic doorway to explore the interior of that cavern. It is of irregular shape, much smaller than the other, but was of more real beauty.

The ceiling was not more than sixty feet high, and was completely visible from the brilliancy of the illumination, supported by natural columns, irregularly placed but all connected by exquisitely fretted arches. These supports were of all colours, red, blue, green, yellow, and purple, nearly transparent. I remained some time in admiration of this magnificent formation, and when I issued from it, Ned had just finished his rude outline. I showed him the 'church' as I called the little cave, and again entered the grand cavern, as the Inca and his escort were ascending a broad flight of steps, having their backs turned toward us. The temptation was too great for Ned to withstand, and, before I could prevent him,—or indeed before I knew what he was about,—he had taken out his 'Revolver' and fired a barrel. The report was instantly followed by a whirring sound in the air, and an immense crystallization, crashed in shivers on the smooth floor right at our feet.

The confusion on the stairs was excessive, for the dignified nobles were alarmed at the tremendous echoes. Helter-skelter they rushed up into a saloon, to which the flight of stairs led, Orteguilla alone remaining upon the steps, and we soon joined him, affecting wonder at the extraordinary report that preceded the fall of the stalactite. We now entered the saloon, and the Inca's escort, finding that no one was hurt, was soon restored to order. The excavated apartment, in which we now were, was furnished with tables, stools, &c., of salt. How tame it looked after the great hall, formed by the hand of nature. Passing through two or more saloons, we entered an entry, and went to the foot of a long staircase which was ascended with much fatigue. A series of three inclined planes, and a long gallery which I thought to be without end, conducted us, at last, to the light of day. In the tent on the plateau, a collation was spread, which was soon demolished, and we returned to the palace, reaching it at half past four in the afternoon, having been eight hours and a half away from it, five of which were spent in the mines. We leave the city at sunrise to-morrow; I, at least, pleased with this visit to the salt-mines, which I would not have missed under any consideration, and which I am afraid, I have occupied too much space in endeavouring to describe.

CHAPTER XXI.

Teman.—The Temple of the Sun at Panonco.—Gopal.—The Temple on the Atolatepec.—Tontam.—Edarallaqua.

MONDAY, December, 13th.—The Inca departed from Xaromba at twenty-minutes of six, and dined, at twelve, in the town of Teman, having arrived there on a fine causeway that skirts the base of the Atolatepec. At three we bent our course towards the south, and in two hours halted in front of the fortified city of Panonco, into which we were instantly admitted.

No sooner had Orteguilla partaken of his afternoon meal, than he came to Ned and me, who were standing, talking, by the fountain in the centre of the apartment, and asked if we would like to visit the Temple of the Sun. We expressed our willingness to do so, and set off immediately. In a few minutes we got to a large square portion of land, railed in with bronze, having two circular stone lodges, and a golden gate between them, which was closed, but, on the appearance of the Inca, it was instantly thrown wide open to admit him and us two, who were his only companions.

At the termination of a long avenue we saw an immense structure in the form of an eight pointed star, all of white marble, and entirely surrounded with a colonnade of the usual shaped pillars. The large octagon, from which the points issue, is twice as high as the rest of the edifice, and its upper part is also surrounded by a row of columns. In the centre of the slightly ascending roof of the octagonal structure is a third range of vase-like pillars, supporting a narrow concave entablature, which is surmounted by a row of marble vases, eighty in number, placed at equal distances.

On approaching this singular erection, I noticed that the points towards the due east and west, were merely porticos, there being no building on them, as upon the six others. We entered by the northern point, and were received by a band of priests, hastily assembled to do honour to the Inca, who is not only the supreme ruler of temporal affairs, but of spiritual ones also. They conducted us through the triangular hall, which is only hung in part with tapestry, the men having been at work putting it up during our visit,—about an hour since.

Dragging some of the workmen's tables out

of the way, the priests gave us admission into the sanctuary, which is a vast eight-sided apartment, with a large skylight of the same shape, in the centre, supported by forty golden columns. From the entablature which these columns support, spring as many more of white marble, which I mentioned in the description of the exterior of the temple. Within the bases of the *interior* columns, is a gold daïs of three steps, in the middle of which is an octagonal altar of porphyry and gold. In the centre of this is the *place* where the cabinet is to stand, but that article is, as yet, unfinished, and consequently not in the sanctuary. The proper vases of the months have not yet made their appearance, and for the time, bronze ones are substituted; the same may be remarked of the vase of Sacrifice on the altar.

In all the other temples I have visited in this valley, the Sun has been represented, invariably, by a disc with rays, placed on the wall behind, and above the altar, but here the peculiar form of the sanctuary has precluded the usual method, and the orb is, consequently, portrayed by an immense gold ball,—whether solid or not, I am unable to state, though I expect that it is merely a shell studded with jewels, and depended over the altar by gold chains which are fastened to the outer edge of the skylight. The eastern and western sides of the sanctuary are open to the the light of day, being all in one with the previously mentioned porticos, separated at night, however, by gilt gates and tapestry. As may be inferred from this description, the temple is not yet completed, but,—as it is the richest in the valley,—there is no doubt but that it will be finished soon. Even in its present state it is the most splendid edifice I have seen since I left the capital city, as I cannot place it before the Council House there. We returned to the palace by seven.

Tuesday, December 14th. To-day our course was again toward the north, as we left Panonco for Atola at an early hour, dining at noon in the city of Gopul, which we did not leave until four, the Inca being obliged to receive the reports of the institutions and the visits of the city authorities. We reached Atola, however, before six, and I have just despatched my portion of supper.

I have not much time to write now, as at nine o'clock, Orteguilla and his escort are going to ascend the Atolatepec, in order to visit a temple, dedicated to the Sun, which has just been finished, and which is already considered the holiest place under Orteguilla's sway, it being the most elevated, and consequently receiving the first rays of the sun every morning. I believe that the Temple is on the uppermost terrace, not on the top of the mountain, which last is perpetually covered with snow, and would not form a very agreeable residence.

We leave Harry Boyd here with the animals and the horse palanquin, as we are to return from the mountain as early to-morrow morning as possible.

Wednesday evening, December 15th. I had scarcely done writing last evening when Grey came in to tell me that the Inca was ready to start, so I put away my journal, came out in front of the palace, got into the litter which had been prepared for me, and started in company with the royal escort. We soon arrived at the foot of the mountain, where every one abandoned their conveyances, and commenced the ascent on foot. This way was easy enough as there was no climbing to be done, merely a succession of terraces, connected by short flights of stone steps. The night was magnificently clear, and it appeared to me that I had never before seen the constellations so distinctly, although the moon was at the full.

As well as I could see in the moonlight, it was twenty minutes past eleven, 'by my *repeater*,' when we reached the park surrounding the New Temple, which being built of the purest white marble, glistened beautifully between the dark green, almost black, trees which overshadowed it. Entering the enclosure we were conducted to the dwelling of the priests, which they had given up for the use of their distinguished visitors, and not being able to accommodate all in this extensive erection, they had pitched tents for the overplus, they themselves spending the night in the Temple.

Ned and I were soon fast asleep, and it appeared to me that five minutes had scarcely passed when we were awakened by a servant, who told us that the 'sun would soon be up.' We arose and dressed ourselves as quickly as we could, and hurried to the Temple. It faces the east, and is oblong in form, the longer sides being the front and back. The façade consists of a deep portico supported by three rows of white marble columns; the entablature over the front range of pillars is concave and narrow, surmounted by twenty-eight good sized vases. The portico is four or five feet lower than the principal building, and this space is occupied by a lattice of the most elaborate richness, that goes around the whole edifice, which, by the way, is crowned by a projecting cornice, of very singular workmanship, ornamented in front, with thirteen marble vases.

There are two entrances under the portico,

placed at each end of the façade, and the northern one admitted us into a large hall, having a broad cornice of gold, from which hangs skyblue tapestry, looped up in thirteen places to display so many oblong niches, in each of which stands a golden vase inscribed with the name of a month. The ceiling is also blue, having a gilt sun in the centre of it. The hall was brilliantly illuminated and filled with priests.

We now entered the sanctuary by a door, or opening, on the left-hand side of the hall. It is a square room draped with blue tapestry, looped up all along the eastern side so as to show the semi-transparent wall of white jaspar, through which the now rising sun began to pour his beams. On the western side are the columns, dais, altar, vases, &c. as in the Temple of the Sun at Geral, and which it is useless to redescribe. Orteguilla officiated as High Priest, and the ceremony over, a splendid breakfast was partaken of in the dwelling of the priests, and the party descended to the city, where it arrived at nine o'clock.

The Inca gave his usual audience for two hours and then departed from Atola in an easterly direction. At four we dined in Tontam, a small town on the west bank of the stream of Naloma, and are now in the city of Edarallaqua, at the foot of the mountain of the same name, in which the gold mines are situated. We shall probably visit them to-morrow, and then proceed to the Fortress of Jacoqulatl, whence we intend to go to Acaposinga from which city we shall return direct to Geral.

CHAPTER XXII.

The Magazines of the Edarallaquatepec.—The Fortress of Jacoqulatl.—Acapcsinga.

THURSDAY December 16th.—Such a day as this has been! Hot as any respectable furnace. But, nevertheless we set off at half past ten this morning, for the mines, which are at least six miles from the palace. It being entirely too warm to be cooped up in our palanquin, Ned and I took up our positions on the backs of our horses, which carried us to our destination in less than two hours and a half, as we had to moderate our speed in order to keep pace with the litters that conveyed the rest of our party.

By the time we reached our destination, Ned and I were nearly smothered by the excessive heat, and could not prevail upon ourselves to enter the mines, well knowing that it must be hotter in there, than where we were. Orteguilla and his escort looked upon us with perfect surprise when we gave our reason for declining to go in; but they went down the shaft without us, allowing us to visit the Magazines during their absence. These are large stone edifices, solidly constructed, fortified, enclosed within a range of high walls and towers, and,—being always lavishly provisioned,—are quite capable of sustaining a siege, which, indeed, I believe they once did from an incursion of the Lambys, or some other wild tribe of Brazil, all the neighbouring ones, in fact, being the inveterate enemies of the valley, which they themselves occupied, previous to the coming of the ancestors of the present inhabitants. This extensive fortress is now garrisoned by only four hundred warriors, who, during our visit, were loitering about the court yards, or basking in the sun, like so many dogs. The Magazines are full of gold ingots, which are *now* sent every *seven* days, to the different cities, in certain quantities, where they are coined for a similar division of thirds to that which I described as taking place at the mint in Geral, except that the Curaças and Nobles get the Inca's share.

Orteguilla did not remain long in the mines, returning perhaps, out of compliment to us, and having partaken of a collation we set out for the city. At four in the afternoon we started for the Fortress of Jacoqulatl, which is eight miles north of Edarallaqua, on the second plateau of the sierra.

It was nearly pitch dark when we arrived there, and the fort could not be made out by the light of the flaring torches carried by the attendants of the escort. There seemed to be a great deal of trouble in getting into it, as we first crossed a bridge, over a moat, I suspect, for I could not see, the moon being obscured by heavy clouds, and then we entered a gate, passing out of another almost at the same moment, issuing once more into the open air. In about three quarters of an hour, after this, we got on another bridge a great deal longer than the first, and passed through a second pair of gates. It was not the fortress yet, as we went again into the darkness of the night. Five minutes more and we entered a large portal, finding ourselves in a proportionably large hall, filled with military officers, and brilliantly illuminated.

I have just demolished my portion of a supper which was prepared for the Inca and his suite, and I am now going to take a good long sleep. I hope to be able to give a description of this fortress to-morrow.

Friday, December 17th.—I awoke at seven, quite frightened at the lateness of the hour. The sun was shining brightly through a window of the clearest jaspar, half shrouded with buff drapery,—and played upon a small fountain that bubbled in the centre of the room. I dressed, and while doing so, went to the window, opened it, and looked out.

My chamber being on the third floor of a tower, I had an extensive view. Close by me were the strong towers and walls composing a portion of the building in which I was; beyond was a wide stone court with a broad causeway leading to a gate in the surrounding walls, which being open, I could see that there was a bridge over a wide moat. On the other side of this, the causeway was continued over a grassy plain,—scattered, here and there, with buildings, perhaps the quarters of some of the garrison,—for about a mile, at which distance there was a second range of walls, and I knew that they were surrounded by water. These outer walls were nearly a mile and a half from my window.

Grey and Harry Boyd now came in, the latter bringing my breakfast, which I made away with in no time, and then went with Ned to pay our morning respects to the Inca, whom we found walking on the walls, attended by several of his suite. We joined him and accompanied the party around the fort, which is of a singular shape.

From a large circular tower,—of a greater height, by the way, than any structure I have seen in the valley, it being, I should suppose, a hundred and fifty feet high, if not more,—diverge four oblong wings, two stories high, and all of the same length, flanked by small square towers. Each of these four buildings terminate in an immense square tower, four stories high, each succeeding story becoming smaller as it ascends. These terminal towers are connected by strong concave walls, interrupted by very small structures, looking like battlements and buttresses.

The view from the top of the central tower, where our walk ended, is, of course, very extended, it being of great height, and also situated on the lower plateau of the northern mountain frontier. Over our heads flaunted the three standards of the Inca,—the principal one is composed of feathers, arranged in stripes of all colours, placed horizontally; the next in point of consideration, is of sky blue cloth with a golden sun, rayed; and the third is black with a full moon embroidered upon it in silver, and surrounded with stars. The two last indicate that in the place over which they float, there is a royal garrison, and the first proclaims the actual presence of the Inca, and is always carried behind him in his progresses.

The two moats surrounding this fortress are supplied by a mountain stream that, after leaping from the plateaus, empties into the Naloma, just before the latter precipitates itself, by a succession of cataracts, into the plain beyond the Sierra.

Orteguilla having made a satisfactory tour of the walls, descended to the magazines, which are full of military stores and provisions. The garrison of this most important fortress numbers over three thousand five hundred men; it has been besieged seven times, taken four, and destroyed once, by the invading tribes, and moreover is constantly in danger of an attack from the same implacable enemies, who never give warning of their intention, but announce themselves before the walls of some town.

We dined at half past eleven, and at noon set out for Acaposinga, where we arrived at seven o'clock this evening, and are quartered in the Palace of the Governor, who is a noble of the Inca race, named Norenoulla.

CHAPTER XXIII.

The Audience Chamber.—Temple of the Moon.—Departure from Acaposinga.—The Canoa.—Gymnasium.

SATURDAY, December 18th. Acaposinga may be the second city in the valley in point of size, but,—if I may be permitted to judge,—it, undoubtedly, would carry off the palm for the greatest dearth of handsome edifices, were it not for the Governor's palace. This redeeming point is most beautiful, and its principal feature is the Audience Chamber, which I will attempt to describe.

It is, at least, four hundred feet long, one hundred and fifty wide, and, at the walls, thirty feet high. I say *at the walls* because at a distance of twenty-five feet from them there are two rows of porphyry columns. Instead of the skylight being directly on the capitals of these, a wall rises on an inwardly inclined angle of about sixty-five degrees, and at a height of sixty feet from the floor is the opening to admit the light, and this is forty feet wide, while the space between the two ranges of pillars is, at the smallest computation, ninety. The skylight is surmounted by a convex entablature, ornamented with a long row of marble vases, and the walls supporting it are draped with white cloth embroidered with gold flowers, while those of the room itself are hung with crimson and gold tapestry. The floor is of polished porphyry, and a double row of large fountains runs the whole length of the apartment between the ranges of columns. The Throne is at the eastern end, under a splendid canopy.

This afternoon Orteguilla took Grey and me to the Temple of the Moon, which is a clumsy looking edifice not far from the governor's palace. It is built of granite; about twenty-four feet high, and sixty square. In the centre of the front is a portico supported by four vase-shaped columns,—and ascended to by means of a flight of eleven steps,—exceeding the height of the remainder of the building by two or three feet, and occupying more than a third of the façade. Twelve feet from the ground is a narrow cornice, beneath which the erection is composed of plain blocks of stone, but above, it projects about three feet, a mass of carving and lattice work to the entablature.

The only entrance is beneath the portico, and the interior of the structure is in not much better taste than the outside. We first entered the hall, which is the width of the portico and thirty feet deep, draped with white cloth, looped up at regular distances to display an underhanging of black. Passing through a wide opening we entered the sanctuary, which occupies the northern half of the building, it is sixty feet long and thirty wide, and entirely hung with black, covered with silver stars. Both ends are open, being merely covered in daytime, by falls of tapestry similar to that on the walls. Opposite to the entrance was a dais, on which stood four altars of basalt sprinkled with silver stars, and over them was a skylight supported by black columns. What struck me most, however, were the representations of the moon, of which there were four, one over each altar,—the two crescents, the half and full moons. They were portrayed by black balls, on which the different stages of the orb were done in silver. On each of the altars stood a square cabinet of silver and a golden vase of sacrifice. There were no vases of the months, and the priests were few in number, while their singing was horrific. We made our escape as soon as possible, fully satisfied that we should not have lost much by remaining in the Palace.

It may be remembered that in the journal of October 12th, I mentioned my having seen 'a cubical monument, about sixteen feet high, seven feet square at the base, and four at the top, of white marble, surmounted by a large silver urn.'* I asked Orteguilla what was the use of this,—as we returned from the Temple,—and learnt that blocks of stone similar to the above described were always erected in commemoration of some great event, such as a birth or death in the royal family, &c., &c. He tells me that there are over seven hundred in the city of Geral alone.

We leave here to-morrow morning for the capital by water, and we therefore sent Boyd by land this afternoon, with the horses, mules, palanquin, and all our quantities of baggage and purchases, the last far out-numbering the former.

Sunday, December, 19th.—Safe at *home* in the palace at Geral after an absence of only ten days! I declare it seems like a month, we have seen so much. We departed from Acaposinga at six o'clock, this morning, in a suite of most superb canoas. The one in which I was, was that appropriated to the Inca, and was about fifty feet long, having at least that number of oarsmen. It was carved out of cedar, with a high prow, richly gilt, and wreathed with beautiful flowers, and over all

*See Chapter XI.

floated the royal banner. At the stern was a pavilion of stained Rhea feathers supported by slight gold columns, with a beautiful carpet on the deck. The cushions and couches were covered with crimson cloth, and thin curtains of some gold woofed material, shaded this eastern looking cabin.

Such was the canoa in which we came up the stream,—a distance of thirty odd miles,—in less than six hours! Thanks to the huge, clumsy looking, triangular sails, that took the place of the rowers as the wind sprung up from the right quarter to waft us on.

On the banks of the Naloma there are many splendid buildings, especially between Acaposinga and Mixocolo, one of which is the Arsenal, as we would call it. The singular disposition of the immense flight of steps,—over three hundred feet long,—the tall flag-staffs around it, and the seven storied tower, looking like a pile of cubical blocks decreasing in size as they rose, struck Ned so forcibly that he obtained permission from Orteguilla to stop the canoa that he might sketch it.

The stream passes through the city of Geral in the form of a canal, both sides of which are ornamented with parks and beautiful residences. At every street the canal is crossed by a bridge, and the only part which is tunnelled is not more than a thousand feet, it being under the promenade on the banks of the lake. We were landed in the park of Orteguilla's palace, and walked from there, having partaken of a collation on board the canoa.

After a long conversation which I held with Grey, this afternoon, we have come to the determination of taking our leave of the valley on Monday the third of January, that is to say, two weeks from to-morrow, all of which time will probably be occupied in preparing. We have not as yet decided which route we shall pursue in order to gain the Atlantic coast, but I think that it is very likely we shall return the same way that we came. We start at the above named period, although it is rather an early one, in order to have plenty of time to get on board a vessel for the United States before the rainy season sets in.

Thursday, December 23rd.—This morning Orteguilla came to the palace, and asked us if we would like to see the Gymnasium ;* and on receiving an answer in the affirmative, he conducted us up the street of the Huaxtepec for six or

* See note on the word "Mint," Chapter XV.

seven blocks, passing the Council House and two of the many public parks in which this city abounds. At length we entered an oblong enclosure, through a magnificent gate. At the eastern and western ends of this park were two long, low edifices of white marble, with large porticos supported by three rows of the vase-shaped columns. These buildings were about seven hundred feet apart, facing each other, (all the intervening space being a level stone pavement,) and having almost the whole of the façades open, only covered, the western by a blue, and the other by a black hanging. Between these erections were two parallel walls, about a hundred feet apart, with the open ends toward the Temples, for such we found the structures to be.

These walls were certainly thirty feet high, exceedingly thick, and over five hundred feet long. At the west end of the northern one, was a small but handsome edifice, of white marble, on a terrace the same height as the wall, ascended to by a flight of stone steps with the usual snaky banisters. On each of the parallel walls, on their inner faces, at a height of not less than twenty feet, projected two stone rings,—some distance apart,—five feet in diameter, and eighteen inches thick, the hole having a diameter of one foot.

Unfortunately for my curiosity, there was no one in the enclosure besides Orteguilla, Ned and myself, so that we could not learn what was the use of these rings, by sight; but the Inca told us that they were used to play a game with balls, the object of which was to throw the ball through the hole, which, he added, was so rarely done, that the fortunate performer was entitled to receive a gold ochol from each person present. Orteguilla told us, also, that the space between the walls was used for athletic exercises by the young commoners of Geral.*

* See Appendix Number One.

CHAPTER XXIV.

New Year's Day.—The Empress's Throne Room.—Her Costume.—Farewell Audience.—Presents.—Departure from the Valley.

SATURDAY, January the first, 1848.—Forty-*eight!* The eight sounds very wrong, and looks so too, for after I had written the date I was called away for an instant, and when I came back, the first thing I saw was the figure 8 staring me in the face. I thought I had made a mistake, and was going to alter it, when I recollected that it was New Year's Day. And a most exquisite day it is; a cool air has been driving some light white clouds from the west, now and then causing them to obscure the sun; and at other times their shadows come flying quickly up the broad streets, in beautiful contrast with the brilliancy of the sunlight. I have heard some superstitious people say that this moving of the clouds was a prognostic of an eventful and sorrowful year, may He avert it from my country!

The birds are singing in the aviary, and the flowers are tossing their perfumed blossoms about in the pleasant breeze. I am not able to write any more to-day, as here comes Ned ready for another extravagant expedition and invasion of shops, which is the way in which we have spent, not only this morning, but the last nine days.

Sunday, 2nd.—This morning we took our solemn farewell of Orteguilla, in the presence of his court, at eleven o'clock; and, by the way, it was a true Irish good-bye, as in the same breath that we bade each other adieu, we mutually promised to meet in the evening, in the Empress's saloons, and as this last mentioned will be the real one, I consider it of more importance than that from which we have just returned.

At eleven o'clock in the evening.—I must describe the Reception Room, and dress of Ahtelaqua, while they are still fresh in my memory.

The former is reached by passing through a suite of twenty splendid apartments, opening into one another, and terminating in that I am going to describe, which is an immense circular saloon, hung with scarlet and gold tapestry, having two rows of columns, alternately of white jaspar and porphyry. Between each of these pillars depended three magnificent golden lamps, and the fountain in the centre of the room was also brilliantly illuminated. The skylight was covered, for the time, with dark blue cloth ornamented with gold stars, and the floor with a crimson carpet, embroidered with bouquets of flowers in their natural colours, on squares of white introduced into the ground work. Large vases of gold, filled with real flowers, tastefully arranged, stood about the floor of this rather too gorgeous apartment, and gold coloured cushions, embroidered with the same precious metal, were piled about the floor.

The throne was placed opposite to the entrance on a dais of seven steps covered with very pale blue, nearly imperceptible from the richness of the silver embroidery. The chair of state is of massive silver, ornamented with precious stones, with splendidly embroidered cushions of lilac and silver, and stands under a canopy of mazarine blue starred with diamonds.

Reposing, rather than sitting, on a couch of blue and silver was Ahtelaqua, for the throne was occupied by Orteguilla. Her white underdress of the finest mull muslin,—Ned and I knew very well where it had come from,—was covered with an embroidery of diamonds and silver; her white bodice was similarly ornamented, as were the hanging sleeves. Her long, ivory-like arms were nearly concealed by the most valuable bracelets, and necklaces of priceless gems were fastened round her throat. Her ear-rings* were massive gold balls encrusted with all sorts of jewels, and and the ruby pendants rested on her rounded shoulders.

But the diamond that adorned the front of her head dress was worthy of her high station. I am convinced that it must weigh over a thousand carats; it is of the first water, and beautifully cut and polished. The plume of white feathers that rose from behind the frame of this gem, had each of the stems set with graduated rubies. At her feet were seated Ineralla and Garoda, while her son Onaméva stood behind her. On the steps of the dais were the young ladies-in-waiting on the Empress and the two princesses, while the remainder of the apartment was filled with nobles and ladies in full dress, positively glowing with jewels.

As we entered, the Royal Family descended from the dais to meet us, and conducted us to the seats which had been prepared for us, on the top of the seventh step, where we held a short conversation, and then took our last,—a very affectionate,—farewell of them. Loaded with costly presents we retreated from the presence, and in

* The ears of both sexes,—of royal rank,—are cut above the lobe when quite young, and are sometimes distended to disgusting length by the heavy ornaments inserted,—for beauty!

the saloons had to bid adieu to our many friends, of both sexes, all of whom pressed upon us some little remembrance of them. We were escorted from one palace to the other by scores of nobles who wished to see all they could of us.

I neglected to mention that this afternoon Ned and I paid a last visit to the Tribunal of Music, the Council House, and several other public buildings which I have before described. And now, although it is nearly midnight, I must go and pack up, as we leave at seven to-morrow.

Monday, January 3d. We took our last, long look at the Palace, at the time above mentioned. The city never appeared more beautiful than when our train of mules wound along the dike amidst the crowd of people who were assembled on it to witness our departure, and as we entered the Fortress of Naloma, I felt quite a choking sensation in my throat, which had an entirely independent cause from an emerald necklace that was fastened there, and which had been thrown to me, by the way, from the top of a house, as I passed from the Street of the Nobles.

Cioaco, Conatzin, Palayn, Onalpo, Mavoga, and a good many other of our friends, accompanied us as far as Ameralqua, where they bade us their final adieu.———

It is needless to dwell on our rapid progress to Quauhtilan, where we arrived at five in the afternoon, entering the walls, which, though they enclosed a great quantity of land, had but a small population within them. One temple in the centre of the *city* was the only place we thought worth visiting, and on doing so decided that it did not repay the trouble.

We tethered our animals in the market-place, and easily found accommodations for ourselves in a private house, as we bore a thread from Orteguilla's borla, which he had given us so that we might obtain anything we were in want of. It proved in this case as powerful as the signet of a despot, which the kind Inca certainly was not.

We spent the night in Quauhtilan and at dawn commenced ascending the terraced sides of the mountain, by which we had first entered the valley; at noon we reached the summit. Looking back, the populous territory of Geral Milco was visible in all its beauty, for a second time, but under different circumstances from those which depended on the former occasion, nearly three months before. Then we were entering, uncertain how we should be received, and at this time we were leaving in full confidence of meeting a cordial welcome should we ever return.

At one we commenced descending the eastern

declivity of the Sierra, and gained the plain, without accident, by sunset. Here we encamped; and after supper decided upon returning by the way of Povoacao and Para, if we could procure a boat at the former place to convey us to the latter.

CHAPTER XXV.

What occurred on the Rout from the Sierra to Povoacao.—A Little too Late.—Povoacao to Angejo.—Conclusion.

EARLY on Wednesday morning we started from the Sierra, and in two hours entered the forest, directing our course towards the east. At night we encamped at the source of the Rio Oteicorolla, after a rather long, and decidedly fatiguing ride, and having supped we made up our fire and retired to rest.

We had not slept long when we were awakened by a wild yell, and found that we were surrounded by savages! Starting to my feet, I seized my 'Revolver,' and fired the six barrels, as quickly as I could; and they were followed by another half dozen from that of Grey, who now brought forward our rifles, while I commenced reloading the pistols. The Indians,—for so I suppose I may call them,—now discharged a flight of arrows and retreated a few steps, evidently alarmed, and leaving several of their comrades on the ground, severely hurt. They would have been killed if we could have seen our enemies distinctly, which we were not able to do, although they stood in the clear moonlight, for our fire was very bright, and they, consequently, could take better aim at us. But their fright from the discharge of the pistols was so great as to prevent them from directing their arrows truly; we could not, otherwise, have escaped unwounded, as we happily did.

Ned extinguished the fire, while I continued to load the fire-arms, and the Boyds to keep up a galling discharge of rifles, which soon dispersed our foes, who fled with horrible yells. We did not pursue them, as we did not wish to leave our baggage and mules at the mercy of any other band that might chance to follow in the track of our late assailants; nor did we feel any particular desire to walk into an ambuscade for the purpose of obliging the savages. We, consequently, kept a watch during the night, but remained undisturbed save by the ravenous musquitoes, who appeared to have a violent wish to rival the Indians in annoying us. They succeeded better, and between the two, none of us were troubled with a superabundant portion of somnolence.

As we were watering our horses, the next morning, preparatory to starting on the day's journey, we were interrupted by a tremendous flight of arrows, none of which, providentially, struck us. Looking in the direction from which we had been thus rudely saluted, we saw a number of savage warriors, scattered through the forest and along the banks of the stream. Mounting our horses, we galloped towards the largest body assembled on the latter, and discharged our pistols. For a moment they were paralysed with fear, caused most probably by our animals, and then, with terrific cries of horror, they took to their heels, disappearing in the dense forest, with the rapidity of thought. We were not troubled by the savages again, but arrived at Povoacao, safe and sound, and without further hindrance of any sort, on the evening of the ensuing Wednesday—January the 12th.

Here we found that there was not a single boat of any sort, the last having sailed two days before, and that there was not the slightest probability of any one coming until after the close of the rainy season. This was provoking, but there was no help for it, and we did not know what to do. It did not suit us exactly to go to the Atlantic coast, by land, nor did we relish any better, crossing the Andes, and proceeding to Lima. Ned and I took a map in order to find some way of getting home, and, after a long consultation, decided upon penetrating eastwardly to the town of Angeja, on the Araquay, opposite the island of Bannanal,—where we were assured that boats could always be procured. There was no time for hesitation, so we packed up again immediately and started at three o'clock on Thursday afternoon, having been only seventeen hours in Povoacao.

Monday, January 17th. We had not gone more than four miles from our last night's camping ground, when the trees suddenly ceased, and a magnificent view presented itself. A plain,—about thirteen miles in length, and three in width, thinly scattered with groups of the gigantic, but graceful, palm, was spread before us,—sweeping up, on the northern and southern sides, into mountains, whose summits were enveloped in clouds. From an elevated plateau of the former range, a mountain torrent sprang down from rock to rock,—looking like a silver thread,—bridged with rainbows, or rather *spray*-bows, and having reached its bed, wound its tortuous way through the plain, a mass of mimic but tumultuous whirlpools. The mountains were piles of immense blocks of stone, whose dull grey colour was,—here and there,—relieved by a cluster of sturdy pines on the higher regions, and of jacaranthas on the lower.

A large number of wild horses were drinking at one part of the stream, while a magnificent jet black animal appeared to be acting as sentinel, for as we issued from the woods, he neighed shrilly, and the rest, throwing up their beautifully shaped heads, joined in chorus with him and bounded off into the forest, which formed the eastern boundary of the valley, with their long manes and tails blowing about in the pleasant breeze.

We got to Angeja on Tuesday morning, January 25th, at half past eleven o'clock, without having met with anything calculated to excite us, save the exquisite scenery through which our long path constantly led us. At this settlement we found quite a presentable sloop which we chartered forthwith, to take us to Para, where we landed, safely in six days that is to say on the first of February.

I have hurried through the last part of my journey, as nothing occurred that is worthy of mention, I being,—unfortunately, perhaps, for my readers, and quite the contrary for myself,—one of those travellers to whom adventures are, 'like angels' visits, few and far between.'

And what is the use of dragging the reader through the dull, monotonous detail of a sea voyage from Para to New Orleans, and thence to Charleston? I answer for myself,—none at all. So I bid,—to all who have tried their powers of patience in order to *get through* this dry production,—what I sincerely hope,—if they do not,—will be but "*au revoir*," not "*adieu*."

A. R. Middletoun Payne.

Wednesday, August 29th, 1849.

APPENDIX.

No. I.

The Tianguez, (Chap. X.); *and Gymnasium,* (Chap. XXIII.)

At the ruins of Chichen Itza in Yucatan, there are the remains of two structures, the uses of which have puzzled many a wiser head than mine. One of these is supposed by many antiquarians, to have been a gymnasium, or tennis court, and it is my pleasant duty to confirm this opinion. The second building,—and that of which I shall first write,—has hitherto been an inexplicable mystery, no one having an idea of what it was originally intended for.

The remains of it are but ill calculated to form a foundation for even antiquarians to build upon, and they are, frequently, clever people, particularly expert in erecting '*Chateaux en Espagne*,' which they do without the slightest provocation or compunction. Palenque, or more properly, *Otolum*, was elevated in the atmosphere for some time by an ingenious person, but all his brother searchers after queer things, piled so much on top of this aerial city, that the whole of it came down, one day, to its proper level, with a grand crash.

But the ruin in question has been found to be in so many little pieces that it has not had the honour of being RESTORED,—as they call it,—although many schemes have been proposed for that purpose. It is an enclosure four hundred feet square, surrounded by four rows of granite piers, which are of all sorts of heights, from seven feet two inches,—the highest I measured in 1838,—down to the slight indentation in the ground where one *has* stood.

Now it is not for a young man like me to *assert* such an important thing, while so very many of the above mentioned old aerial architects have cogitated upon it for such a length of time without coming to any conclusion, and, therefore, I must content myself by *inquiring*,—Is not this incomprehensible, unelevatable, unrestorable ruin, the remains of a market place? The absence of any slabs of granite that might have served as part of a roof, may be easily accounted for, as although the Tianguez in Geral had a stone ceiling, that at Acaposinga was roofed with cedar beams and palm leaves.

To turn to the Gymnasium. In this case there

is nothing to prove, the dispositions of the details of both being precisely the same at Geral and at Chichen Itza. The Temple at each end, the raised edifice for the judge of the games, and the thick parallel walls are the same in both, only varying in size, and in the dedication of the Temples,—at Geral to the Sun and Moon, and at the other to some of their outlandish gods.

APPENDIX.

No. 2.

The New Calendar.—(Chapter XVII.)

THE names of the days of the month are:—

Ac, Chi-ac, Mal-ac, Hun-ac, Oll-ac, Kab-ac, *Der*-ac,	comprising 1st week.
En, Chi-en, Mal-en, Hun-en, Oll-en, Kab-en, *Der*-en,	" 2d "
Ila, Chi-ila, Mal-ila, Hun-ila, Oll-ila, Kab-ila, *Der*-ila, . . .	" 3d "
Cum, Chi-cum, Mal-cum, Hun-cum, Oll-cum, Kab-cum, *Der*-cum, . .	" 4th "

The thirteen months have each twenty-eight days with the exception of Memib, which is now the last month of the year. It has always twenty-nine days,—the 29th being called Eneda,—and on leap-year it has a thirtieth known as Bajeca.

The days of our months, upon which the Geralian months commence, are as follows:—

1.	Olab	on	June 9th.
2.	Canno	"	July 7th.
3.	Malan	"	August 4th.
4.	Cop	"	September 1st.
5.	Xoo	"	September 29th.
6.	Ziña	"	October 27th.
7.	Naon	"	November 24th.
8.	Pavan	"	December 22d.
9.	Quiloo	"	January 19th.
10.	Kamem	"	February 16th.
11.	Geb	"	March 16th.
12.	Alac	"	April 13th.
13.	Memib	"	May 11th.

The above list is not made for a leap year, as then, Geb would begin on March 15th, Alac on April 12th, and Memib on May 10th.

APPENDIX.

No. 3.

The following is the list of the state of the thermometer as I noticed it from October 11th to the 1st of January.

Day of the Week.	Month.	Day of the Month.	Time. H.	Time. M.	Thermometer.
Monday,	October	11	3	6	88°
Tuesday,	"	12	1	40	87°
Wednesday,	"	13	12		90°
Thursday,	"	14	1	10	88°
Friday,	"	15	1	7	94°
Saturday,	"	16	1	38	78°
Sunday,	"	17	1	50	75°
Monday,	"	18	3	9	98°
Tuesday,	"	19	2	30	96°
Wednesday,	"	20	12	25	87°
Thursday,	"	21	3	18	94°
Friday,	"	22	1	6	91°
Saturday,	"	23	12	43	83°
Sunday,	"	24	2	12	88°
Monday,	"	25	4	27	84°
Tuesday,	"	26	1	12	76°
Wednesday,	"	27	3	42	87°
Thursday,	"	28	2	9	80°
Friday,	"	29	12	13	81°
Saturday,	"	30	1		89°
Sunday,	"	31	3	50	94°
Monday,	November,	1	2	20	90°
Tuesday,	"	2	1	39	83°

Day of the Week.	Month.	Day of the Month.	Time. H.	Time. M.	Thermometer.
Wednesday,	November,	3	12	25	97°
Thursday,	"	4	3	46	99°
Friday,	"	5	12		78°
Saturday,	"	6	12		83°
Sunday,	"	7	3	16	95°
Monday,	"	8	1	25	88°
Tuesday,	"	9	2	48	92°
Wednesday,	"	10	12	30	76°
Thursday,	"	11	1	6	85°
Friday,	"	12	1	18	84°
Saturday,	"	13	3	15	97°
Sunday,	"	14	2	30	89°
Monday,	"	15	1	12	77°
Tuesday,	"	16	12	40	90°
Wednesday,	"	17	12	15	99°
Thursday,	"	18	3	10	99°
Friday,	"	19	3	25	106°
Saturday,	"	20	3	40	98°
Sunday,	"	21	2	16	93°
Monday,	"	22	12	50	79°
Tuesday,	"	23	3	13	104°
Wednesday,	"	24	1	9	91°
Thursday,	"	25	12	40	84°
Friday,	"	26	2	8	78°
Saturday,	"	27	2	14	85°
Sunday,	"	28	3	12	99°
Monday,	"	29	12	30	76°
Tuesday,	"	30	1	45	89°
Wednesday,	December,	1	3	6	108°
Thursday,	"	2	1	30	94°
Friday,	"	3	12	25	80°
Saturday,	"	4	2	40	95°
Sunday,	"	5	1	54	72°
Monday,	"	6	12	10	87°
Tuesday,	"	7	3	15	93°
Wednesday,	"	8	3	50	105°
Thursday,	"	9	1	28	99°
Friday,	"	10	3	45	89°
Saturday,	"	11	12	6	71°
Sunday,	"	12	1	25	88°

Day of the Week.	Month.	Day of the Month.	Time. H.	Time. M.	Thermometer.
Monday,	December,	13	2	30	76°
Tuesday,	"	14	1	12	94°
Wednesday	"	15	3	45	101°
Thursday,,	"	16	3	27	114°
Friday,	"	17	3	9	100°
Saturday,	"	18	12	15	85°
Sunday,	"	19	2	8	94°
Monday,	"	20	1	35	89°
Tuesday,	"	21	12	45	77°
Wednesday,	"	22	3		97°
Thursday,	"	23	3	16	106°
Friday,	"	24	1		92°
Saturday,	"	25	2	30	96°
Sunday,	"	26	2	45	98°
Monday,	"	27	2		94°
Tuesday,	"	28	3	18	110°
Wednesday,	"	29	3	15	105°
Thursday,	"	30	12	30	86°
Friday,	"	31	3	43	97°

SUPPLEMENT

TO THE

GERAL-MILCO.

BY

A. R. MIDDLETOUN PAYNE.

INTRODUCTION

TO

SUPPLEMENT.

IT is now full two years since I completed the foregoing portion of this volume; but all those kind friends who have done me the honour to read it, in its manuscript form, protest against its shortness, and have thus persuaded me to commence a few supplementary chapters on the manners and customs of the Valley of the Incas, in order to increase its length.

I cannot even expect them to prove other than dry and tedious to many readers, for as this appendix is to be written far from the Valley, and chiefly from recollection and a few hieroglyphical works, the labour of translating these has deprived me of all that enthusiastic excitement under the influence of which the first part of the work was written.

A. R. MIDDLETOUN PAYNE.

September 19th, 1851.

PART SECOND.

CHAPTER I.

Government, Revenue, Military and Civil Institutions, etc.

In treating upon such important subjects, it is perhaps scarcely proper for me to judge merely by the personal experience of an eighty days' residence, but some excuse may exist in the fact of my being the first traveller to penetrate into the Valley of Geral, and make any stay within it. Notwithstanding the short space of time which Grey and myself remained the guest of the hospitable descendants of the ancient Peruvians, it must be acknowledged that we had remarkable facilities afforded us to notice the working of the machinery of state, by our daily intercourse with its sole director, the Inca Orteguilla; travelling with him, residing in his palaces, the private audience chambers always open to us, even when closed against the High Priest of the Sun himself; entertained by him in private and in public; and visited by him, without ceremony, at all hours. But of course even this unrestrained communion could not place in our possession all the knowledge necessary for a correct delineation of the minute ramifications of the government throughout the Incalate, to obtain which we have been obliged to resort to the hieroglyphical manuscripts of the country, which were easily procured though not so easily read.

We beg, therefore, that it may be understood our principal authorities for this first chapter,—and indeed the greater part of the volume,—are the three following,—"The True History of the Incalate, by Loverca of Acaposinga," "The Government of Geral, by Caonaga of Nalava," and "The Institutions of Geral by Valaïon of Nalava." These writers are all *amataus* in the great college of the Capital, and are probably the best authorities to be found, certainly the most modern that we could obtain, as they were all issued during our stay in Geral. The work of Valaïon is the most extensive of the three as regards the subjects treated of, and its size; it covers in its hieroglyphic form, two hundred and thirty seven folds, or pages, each seven inches long by twelve in width; the character in which it is written is small and extremely legible, and the composition very fluently worded, being by far the best specimen of Geralian literature that I have as yet met with amongst my very large collection. The other two works are much smaller, scarcely numbering seventy five folds between them; the 'History of the Incalate' having but twenty-two, and the 'Government of Geral' forty nine. This last is more like a code by which to guide the state, than a book for the information of the public, and as such is extremely minute in all its details in regard to the legislation of both civil and military and religious affairs, being precisely the thing for my purpose, and I render thanks to the Amatau Caonaga for having written it.

To begin then. The Government of Geral is an hereditary absolute monarchy, the Inca being the State, the head of all military, civil and religious institutions; from him emanate all laws, they being ratified by the Council of Nobles, the power of which assembly is altogether nominal, not only from reverence to the Inca, who is looked upon as the Son of the Sun, but also from a total incapacity to act, being unorganized and not permitted to think for itself. The Inca is a despot,—whether tyrannical or not depends *considerably* upon his natural character,—whose edicts are uncontrovertible, save by himself. Next to him are three dignitaries, the High Priest of the Sun, the Commandant of Acaposinga, (the head of the military forces,) and the President of the Valley, who is the grand master of police and also the supreme judge in matters of legislative power. Under the High Priest of the Sun are the High Priests of the various cities of the Incalate, who rule over all the temples in their respective diocesi; each temple has its Vicar General, who, in his turn, oversees the conduct of the priests and neophytes, and is responsible to the High Priest of his diocess for all the misdemeanors of his underlings. Then there are the convents of the priestesses and novices, under the superintendence of the High Priest of the Sun himself, without any intermediate power, save that of the individual Vicaress Generals. He holds his court at Geral, and makes an annual tour through the Incalate to inquire into grievances, in company with the Inca, or Supreme Head of the Church, who consecrates all the temples finished since the previous year's visit. One of the principal officers under the High Priest of the Sun is the Overseer of the Temples, whose duty it is to see that all the religious edifices in the valley are built in accordance with the laws laid down by the founder of the dynasty.

I now turn to the military department, whose

head—under the Inca—is the Commandant of Acaposinga, holding his court in that city, which is the great arsenal of the Incalate. Under him are the military governors of the different cities and fortresses, and the Master of the Arsenals, an important personage who has the inspection of all the storehouses in the valley, each of which has a resident inspector to keep it in order. All the military governors taken together form a Court Martial, before which are tried all offences against the discipline of the army, which is, as a whole, divided in bodies or squares—as they are called—of fifty men, the fiftieth being its commander, and preserver of its conduct. A division commanded by a captain, consists of eight of these squares, two captains and their troops being quartered in every city and fortress, under the control of its governor. A square of soldiers is stationed at every arsenal, under the command of the Resident Inspector, and these various bodies are moved about at the order of the Commandant of Acaposinga, under the Inca's sign manual.

The third department of the government is the civil, beneath the direction of the President of the Valley, who, in his capacity of Judge, has two associate Judges, one for the northern and one for the central district of the Valley, who have under them a Judge for every city in their portion of the Incalate; these again have numerous subordinate magistrates in every village, town and community, dispensing justice to a certain number of people. The population of the Valley, in the aggregate, is divided into parties of ten families, the head of the tenth being the overseer of the duties of all the others; every five of these parties are supervised by one of the above mentioned magistrates, who keeps a register containing the names, age, sex, occupation and wealth of every individual in the fifty families beneath his care. Of this register three duplicates are made, one to be forwarded to the judge of the city, another to the district judge, and the third to the President of the Valley, which last is placed in the care of the Officer of the Rolls, who can at any moment give the precise population of the Valley, the average age and wealth; the distribution of labour is apportioned by these rolls.

The President of the Valley has also under his orders the civil governors of the cities, who have all power concerning matters of police, establishing officers similar to our sheriffs, who rule over the subordinate officials who preserve the public tranquillity, by arresting all the disturbers of it: these are arraigned before the sheriffs, and on condemnation are sentenced, for a time proportioned to their offence, either to serve in the army or labour in the state works. Incendiarism, robbery, brawling on the highway, and assault and battery, are punishable in this way; but if this last offence, or that of incendiarism, prove the cause of the death of any one, the criminal is sentenced to solitary confinement in one of the state prisons. Murder and homicide, with crimes of that class, are expiated by strangulation; but such cases are extremely rare, and are tried by the district judges in person, aided by the civil governor of the place in which the deed was committed.

The Councils on War, on Domestic Affairs, and on the State of the Temples, are composed of the Inca, the High Priest of the Sun, the Commandant of Acaposinga, and the President of the Valley.

This is all that I deem necessary to state on the subject of government, turning next to the sources of revenue, and its distribution.

There are no taxes, no foreign commerce, and consequently no tariff; the revenue therefore consists of the products of the mines, quarries, plantations, manufactories, and principally, in the ownership of the immense droves of llamas that roam the upper plateaus of the mountains, tended by numerous shepherds in the payment of the government. No person is permitted to own a single one of these invaluable animals save the State, unless by special edict of the Inca, who frequently grants the right of possessing them to some of the private manufactories of woollen cloths.

The mines are the greatest source of revenue, and are of gold, silver and copper; the first of these are situated in the Edarallaquatepec, the whole of which is deeply impregnated with the precious ore. It is also taken in enormous quantities from the bed of a small stream issuing from the mountains of Pocotatl,—the western boundary of the Valley,—which are also mined to a great extent. The course of the stream is semi-annually altered, being six months in its natural channel, and the remainder of the year in an artificial one, constructed parallel to the former; when the water is turned from one of these, the ensuing half year is employed by the workmen in removing the lumps of gold from the clefts in the rocks, where it has been deposited by the water since the last operation, and thus a continual harvest is gathered, which is refined in the large workshops, close at hand, melted, cast into ingots, and despatched every twenty days to the capital, where it is coined as I have previously detailed.

The silver mines must be, according Valaïon,

very remarkable, and had we known of their singularity we most assuredly would have visited them. The ore is so pure that it is chiseled out, as in the mine of Huantajaya, in lumps of various sizes, and it is unnecessary to refine it, the act of melting it being sufficient to drive off all its impurities. These profitable "diggins," exist within the walls of the capital, in the Huaxtepec, upon whose terraces Grey and I have often promenaded, unknowing what we could have seen within the hill.

The copper can scarcely be said to be mined but rather quarried, as the excavation has been commenced at the surface and carried down to a depth of two hundred feet and more, at the base of the mountain of Imamba, named after a small town situated in the extreme north-western corner of the Valley, not more than ten miles from the city of Xaromba. Valaïon writes that this portion of the Incalate has been rendered unhealthy, and unfruitful by the opening of this mine, which can be accounted for probably by the presence of a "great quantity of yellowish dust," which he subsequently mentions as being precipitated by the action of the fire in the kilns where a portion of the copper ore is melted and cast into ingots. This dust is, of course, sulphur. Another part of metal is pressed and rolled into plates for manufacturers.

All these mines are worked to the utmost extent by the government and their products come direct to the capital, where they are divided in certain proportions between the mint and the Tianguez, in the first of which places the metal is coined, and in the second sold to the highest bidder. The money thus produced is deposited in the mint and distributed in a manner to be described further on.

The great salt mines of the Atolatepec form another item to swell the revenue; their products are immense, and are disposed of at the mountain itself, carried away by the wholesale purchasers to retail in their respective cities.

All the stone quarries in the Valley are the property of the government, which sells the marble, jasper, etc., to the different customers, realizing considerable profit as may be imagined, most of the men employed being offenders against the law.

The manufactories of cotton and woollen cloths, of bronze articles, furniture, &c., are also productive, but not so much so as the items we have previously mentioned, there being no monopoly in these wares; but their inferiority is balanced by the plantations of cotton, sugar, rice, maize, barley, wheat, beans and yams. These are in the possession of the government only, and are of immense extent, spread over the terraces of the mountains and on the plains of the valley affording an unfailing source of revenue. The products of these plantations are stored in huge magazines, scattered over the country, and sold to the people by the resident inspectors, who transmit their receipts semi-annually to the capital to unite with the rest of the revenue, which is divided as a whole into three perfectly equal portions, one which is devoted to the Inca, as his private purse, another to the Sun, and the third to the payment of salaries.

The Inca disburses his third in the erection of palaces, public buildings, manufactories, &c., and in the support of his harem and very large family, each individual having a certain annuity. The nobles of the valley are included in this, as they are all blood relations of the reigning sovereign, and are consequently interested in maintaining his rights against any aggressor.

The third of the revenue appropriated to the Sun, is devoted to the sustenance of the priests, convents, temples and consistories, and to the erection of new temples; while the salaries of the innumerable officers and employees of the government nearly swallow up the remaining portion, the surplus being placed away for future wants.

The population of the valley in 1847, was 2,815,070, of which, 1,664,000 resided in the capital city, Acaposinga having 231,564 inhabitants; Tezcatl 142,362; Xaromba 75,623; and the remaining 701,491 being scattered through the towns and villages of the country. This number of persons residing in a space of 3600 square miles, rather less than more,—gives an average of $781\frac{17}{18}$ to a square mile, more than double in density the population of Belgium, which is the thickest inhabited extent of country in Europe. The average length of life is a few weeks over 53; diseases are rare, and are principally fevers of not very malignant character.

Over 200,000 persons are employed in the mines and quarries, and nearly as many more in the construction of the public works, while the army enrolls 47,600 men, 2000 of whom form a part of the population of Geral, and 4000 more reside in Acaposiñga. Some 20 or 30,000 persons are engaged in tending the vast droves of Llamas and Vicuñas. The rest of the population consists of artizans, farmers, weavers, and merchants or shopkeepers.

The actual revenue of the valley is almost fabulous in its enormous amount, bordering very close upon six hundred millions of our dollars, to follow Valaïon's estimate, and eight hundred millions according to Caonaga's, which is rather too vast for belief even when we remember, that it comprises nearly all the specie in the Incalate.

Having finished this portion of my projected task, I proceed to speak of the accommodations for travelling and transportation throughout the country, a subject of sufficient importance to have a short chapter to itself.

CHAPTER II.

Modes of Communication.

NOTHING can be better than the splendid roads, or rather causeways, that traverse the Geral-Milco in every direction, connecting every city, town and village with the great capital from which it derives its support, and rendering every facility for travel. These vast causeways are composed entirely of rough hewn stone, cut only at the edges, where they are bevelled and connected so beautifully with the surrounding blocks that the juncture is scarcely perceptible:—they are at least twenty feet wide, the surface being of a sort of gravel, rolled smooth and kept in the most perfect order. A parapet about eighteen inches high extends along each side of the road, which is carried on a railroad-like level over and through every apparent obstacle, without any deviation from a straight line, which, although undeniably the very reverse of romantic, is at the same time very agreeable to the traveller and his animals, shaded as he is by a double row of thick foliaged trees, planted on each side of the highway, interspersed with jets of water and fruit-trees, whose offerings are at the service of every passer by. Every two or three miles along these routes, is a small stone dwelling, with an enclosed space of ground, tenanted by several men holding the office of chasquis, or postmen, and at less intervals, small clusters of houses form the homes of the numerous palanquin bearers, earning their livelihood by carrying travellers from one station to the next: eight of these consider themselves well rewarded in receiving a single silver ochol, (62½ cents.)

Almost all the travelling is performed in litters, the richer nobles being carried by their own servants, and the less affluent of the class by the palanquin bearers above mentioned. The wealthy citizens do the same, but the poorer orders make use of the lines established by the government, which are wheeled conveyances holding four persons, sometimes six, drawn by a train of ten or twelve llamas harnessed three abreast, with a driver who walks at the head of the line. Several of these *maraconas* leave every town of any size early in the morning, and are very well patronized, the fare being quite reasonable, and the rate of progression but little slower than that of the palanquins. Multitudes of people throng the capital city on the annual festival of the sun, to behold the magnificent ceremonies of the great temple, which take place in the middle of summer, and which I did not, in consequence, have an opportunity of witnessing. At that period of the year,—writes Departesa of Xaromba, (another of my authorities,) in his "Geralian Manners,"—the causeways are crowded with palanquins and maraconas, hundreds of which daily enter the capital, discharging their freights, and returning immediately for more passengers. During the three days which the festival lasts, the population of the city is nearly doubled, for every family in the valley sends one or more representatives to participate in the annual celebration. These new comers are lodged either with their relations, or in the immense *coralans* that abound throughout the capital. A *coralan* is somewhat like an eastern khan, as every guest provides his own meals, nothing being furnished by the proprietors but the sleeping places, which have mattresses composed of a peculiar kind of moss, similar to that known to us by the name of South Carolina moss, admirably suited for such a purpose.

The transportation of the products of the mines and quarries, is effected by the means of a square cart, having four very large wheels, composed of the wood of the *cecropia peltata*, or trumpet tree, tired with bronze. These conveyances, called *lalamas*, are of great capacity and strength, and are drawn by a long train of llamas, who perform the journey from the mines of the Edarallaquatepec to Geral,—a distance of fifty-one miles,—in thirteen hours, which is quite quick for such seemingly weak animals, the loads frequently weighing two or three hundred weight. Lalamas are used also to convey the baggage of weathy travellers, but principally for the purposes above mentioned, though for the transportation of large bronze manufactures, and other bulky commodities, they are much employed.

Cotton, woollen and similar merchandise, the products of the woods and fields, is generally carried across the country packed carefully on the backs of llamas, who can bear a burden of from 200 to 250 pounds, without inconvenience. Long trains of these animals, heavily laden, are constantly to be met on the highways, attended by their numerous drivers, and followed, in most cases, by a superintendent in his litter.

There are numerous descriptions of palanquins; *loca-dals*, used for travelling; *ena-dals*, employed in passing through the streets; *fomer-dals*, in shopping or visiting; and the *posei-dals*, which are devoted to the occupations of the ladies. These four kinds are double or single, and a very few of the first mentioned are made to accommodate four persons, in which case, however, they cannot be said to come under the head of litters, as they are suspended between eight wheels, and drawn by llamas.

The single loca-dal is about eight feet long, four wide, and four high, lined with thick cushions, and having a mattress on the floor, upon which the traveller reclines at his ease, and reads, or enjoys the prospect from the latticed openings which are placed all along the upper half of the sides. These windows are provided with curtains, to regulate the light at the option of the occupant. A little table can be formed by raising a flap pendant against one of the sides, and a set of small drawers are placed at the foot of the palanquin, with a closet over them, in which edibles are placed. The double loca-dal is similar to the single, save that it is nearly six feet wide; and is borne by eight men instead of four.

The *ena-dal* is only four feet long, three wide, and five high, in short, an oblong box placed on its smaller end, and furnished with a comfortable seat; the sides are usually solid only to the height of two feet, the rest being open to the air, with a roof supported by four slender columns placed at the corners. Sometimes it is latticed and curtained, but not often. It is carried by four servants,—when double by eight,—and admittance is afforded by a door on each side.

The fomer-dal strongly resembles the last, differing only in the method of bearing: the first has the handles placed underneath, and is consequently mounted high in air, on the shoulders of its bearers, while the fomer-dal, like the loca-dal, has its handles placed near the top, and is therefore elevated but a few inches above the ground. It has the back and front solid to the roof, with the exception of two small circular openings, through which the occupant sees where he wishes to go, and transmits his orders to the carriers. The sides are open, but it is considered very inelegant to pass your head out of these, and, in fact, I never saw any one commit such an infraction of decorum.

These three descriptions of palanquin are confined solely to the use of males, if we except the double locadal, in which ladies also travel when they venture to leave the city of their residence, which is a rare occurrence: but they have a peculiar kind of litter devoted to their especial use, called the Poseidal, which closes the list. It is six feet in length, four wide and high, closed at both ends to the roof, the sides being composed of delicate lattice work lined with gauze, and impenetrable to the view from the outside, while from the interior every thing can be seen with perfect distinctness. Within, these conveyances are padded and provided with numerous soft square cushions upon which recline the fair occupants,—for these litters always carry two,—while on the exterior they are gilded and painted according to the taste of the owner. They are borne on the shoulders of four attendants, by as many long handles,—extending from the upper corners of the palanquin,—which are very often carved like snakes, and richly ornamented.

The Inca always uses (except on his annual tours through the Valley) a litter of peculiar form being a richly gilt frame something resembling a chair, cushioned and shaded by a magnificent canopy of variously coloured feathers, intermingled with long jewelled pendants, supported by four long poles, so crossed as to form a square with eight projecting handles. On the square is placed the chair and canopy, and each of the handles is held by two nobles of the highest rank. An ornamented piece of wood, something like a dash board on a small scale, is placed before the chair, for the Inca to rest his feet against, and when moving along the streets, the uppermost peak of the canopy is, at least, fifteen feet from the ground.

So much for land travelling and means of communication, and there is but little to be said of river craft, as the streams are mostly too small for navigation, the Naloma, and one of its tributaries,—before mentioned as flowing from the mines of Pocotatl,—being the only water courses on which boats are to be found. The products of these mines are brought to Geral in large canoas, with from twenty to thirty oars, and military stores are also transported to and from Acaposinga by water, and some merchandize is occasionally to be met ascending and descending the stream, between that city and the capital, but not further east, as the rapids commence a few miles below.

The nobles and rich inhabitants of Geral possess pleasure canoas in which they take a view or sail on the canal that passes through part of the capital. This canal connects the lake of Naloma with the lakes on the upper plateaus of the Sierra Paricis, and is a natural formation, artificialized by the natives having lined its banks with polished stone from the former body of water to the point where the stream enters the Inca's park, through which it flows in its untortured way. In its passage through the city it is crossed by innumerable draw bridges of simple, though strong construction, which I have described in the first part of this book, while at its junction with the Lake of Naloma there is a splendid triumphal *arch!* not, however, a perfect curve, but consisting of two arcs united by a flat slab, while the outer coating is in steps.* It was built two hundred years ago, in commemoration of the completion of the canal by the Inca, Huayna Evora, and is in excellent preservation, being composed of huge blocks of stone. It is about three hundred and fifty feet from the lake, the canal being entirely covered over, for this distance, by the continuous bridge that unites the western and eastern portions of the wide quay which extends all around the lake.

The state barges of the Inca and his suite, I have also previously attempted to portray, and need, therefore, speak only of the small canoas in which a party of two or three, takes an evening's amusement on the bosom of the grand canal. They are narrow boats, some twenty feet in length, guided by a single boatman, and having a little cabin, tastefully ornamented, placed amidships, much resembling in their general form, the Venetian Gondola, excepting in the brilliantly coloured

*An arch of this description still exists nearly perfect at Labrà, in Yucatan. The one above mentioned is similar in every respect, except being much more lofty.

curtains that fall into the water from the latticed openings that serve to light the interior of a cabin, fitted up with barbaric magnificence. Many a time, and oft, have Grey and I, with one of our princely friends, glided over the calm surface of the lake in one of these charming skiffs, to some of the many floating islands (Chinampas,) thence to take a moonlight view of the gorgeous City of the Inca; or darted through the tunnel to the canal, emerging from the silence of the former into the deafening laughter and chatter of the crowds that filled the canoas, and thronged the stone banks of the latter.

CHAPTER III.

Buildings:—Materials, Style, Solidity, &c.

No sensible person can possibly suppose, even for an instant, that, in the revolution of three centuries and more, no improvement was made by the Geralians upon the modes of constructing edifices, employed by their ancestors,—the Peruvians and Mexicans,—for in the history of all nations, we find the founders residing in huts of branches plucked from the surrounding trees, and rudely piled together to form a shelter from the changes of the weather. Look to the early traditions of the most refined of ancient nations:—while its true origin is undiscernible through the misty darkness of long passed years, we find its inhabitants, on the arrival of Inachus, from Egypt,—living in caves, in the lowest depths of barbarism. To what eminence they attained in architectural science is well known to every one. The Peruvians and Mexicans, in all probability likewise commenced by living in artificial caves, thence to improve in skill, until they erected the immense palaces and temples, whose remains are strewn over modern Peru and Central America, rivalling in their dimensions and grandness of conception, the proudest monuments of modern art. To what greater dexterity they would have arrived in their native land is unknown, for the successful invasions of the Spanish pirates, effectually checked all further advancement on the part of the subdued natives, reducing them to a state of absolute servility.

The Geralians had, therefore, every advantage for rapid improvement, starting into a distinct existence from a chance union of two nations, renowned for their advanced civilization, at the turning point of their greatness; carrying with them all the arts and sciences, which were the offspring of centuries of previous experience, and an enterprising spirit of their own, that prompted them to make a last stand for freedom in the wilderness of Brazil.

Instead, therefore, of the new nation's first house being a rude construction of leaves, we find the founders building a magnificent palace of wrought stone, (in the intermingled taste of Mexico and Peru,) for the residence of their Inca, with huge exterior flights of steps guarded by the symbolic serpents of the northern country, and decorated with the golden disks that manifested the religion of the warmer clime; in short the very edifice of which a description has already been given,—in which I, the reader's humble servant, was lodged by order of the Inca.

The duty which devolves upon me, is to show the present state of the architecture of the valley, and to do so I will commence by treating of the materials principally employed, which are five in number, white and black marble, brown stone, granite, and a stone of a pale buff colour, much used and capable of receiving a high polish, while it is susceptible of the finest carving. In interior finishing, jasper, agate, pictorial marble,—which is scarce and very highly prized,—a species of verde antico, and a light red coloured marble with which walls are sometimes faced.

Entire rooms are sometimes lined with sheets of amber, or lapis lazuli, the former being occasionally made into hollow columns, the plates being joined by rings of silver, and in these are placed lights, producing a very singular appearance. I remember a store in the street of the Ocelot that had a portico supported by four pillars of this description, which I used frequently to admire during my short residence in that thoroughfare.

In both public and private buildings of any

pretension, a great quantity of carving is to be found, very beautifully executed, of scrolls, birds, and men in high relief. The columns are of a vase-like form, as I have many times mentioned in the foregoing journal, with capitals much resembling those found in the old temples of Hindoostan, being in the form of circular cushions, apparently crushed nearly flat by the weight of the superincumbent mass of transverse beams. The contour of the shaft,—if I may so term it,—is more elegant, slight and graceful than those of the East Indies, but a very great similarity can be traced between them.

What we designate as the Gothic arch is known, and employed much more extensively than the Norman or semi-circular, which I saw used merely on the banks of the canal in Geral, where a few houses, abutting upon the water, have them in their lower stories over the foot of a flight of steps,—leading to the first floor,—used by the occupants in descending to their canoas: even in such cases, a semi-oval arch is more common.

This is a manifest improvement upon the ancient architecture of America, as the only approach to an arch to be found among the numerous remains as yet explored, is at Labnà—mentioned by Stephens in his 'Yucatan,'—where there is a gateway formed of two slight arcs whose point of intersection is cut off by a horizontal slab,—a description tallying exactly with that given in the last chapter of the Triumphal Arch of the Inca Huayna Evora at Geral. In one of the corridors in the palace Palenque (Central America) there are small openings to admit light, in the form of a semicircular cusped arch, but these are hewn out of a single block, not formed of numerous stones: windows similar to this I have met with often in different parts of the valley.

In the erection of all buildings the first thing done is to dig to the depth of two or three feet, the level surface thus produced being pounded and rolled as firmly as possible, after which the space is refilled with solidly cemented masonry. On this terrace, which in some cases is carried as much as four or five feet above the street, the structure is gradually raised to the desired elevation, seldom more than two stories unless it be a storehouse or large mercantile wareroom. The walls are by law prohibited from being thinner than fifteen inches for private houses of one story, than twenty-one if more, and those of the magazines are never less than thirty.

The residences of the wealthy citizens of Geral,—for the nobles live in perfect palaces, so nearly resembling the previously given description, that I omit mentioning them in this place, —are generally surrounded by a garden, fronting some principal street, from which a wide and smoothly rolled gravel path leads to the *Z'ilathal*, or portico of the house, which is generally supported by columns, and which,—in two story buildings,—does not protrude from the façade, but is enclosed by the surrounding apartments, and is very much like a room with one side removed, as it is furnished with ottomans and tables, while from the centre of the ceiling hangs the great *Uthirb-ilathal*, or Lamp of Welcome, a large and not inelegant article composed of delicate lattice work in gold, or some less valuable metal, surrounded with long tassels pendent from a projecting frame that forms as it were the cornice of the chandelier. A door in the centre of the Z'ilathal admits the visitor into a long hall on one side of which is the Egarathon, or parlour, where the host receives, and on the other is the Ovvaidon or eating room. The first is generally square, and has at one end a raised dais of two steps called the *Tarim-ilathal* (Place of Welcome,) on which the master of the house sits, and whence he converses with his visitor, to receive whom, he rises. It is a great favour if he descend the two steps, and still higher honoured is the guest who is met half way, for a seat on the Tarim-ilathal is sure to be offered for his acceptance. The whole room is often greatly decorated; either the walls are richly carved, covered with valuable marble, or else hung with tapestry of the utmost magnificence. Communicating with the Egarati on is the private room of the owner, where he instructs his younger children, makes up his accounts, has interviews with his master of ceremonies, and receives his most intimate friends. Opening into this is his *Evoridua* or sleeping apartment, and a passage that leads to the second floor, if there is one, otherwise the rooms about to be mentioned extend further back on the same level with those already described. The *Avvaroga* or apartments of the women, consist of chambers, a nursery for the children, and a sitting room where the ladies either spin, embroider, read, or in other ways employ themselves. Here also are found large presses where are kept the dresses of the family, and chests in which are secured the table linen and plate, which after every meal are brought to the mistress of the house. No male may enter the Avvaroga save the master of the house, such of his friends as he wishes to present to his family, and the head servant.

While all strangers are thus excluded from the private parts of the mansion, they are freely admitted into the rooms on the other side of the entrance hall, which are first the *Uvvithon*, or pantry; next to which, and on a line with it, is the *Ovvaidon*, or eating-room, behind which is the *Itanalpa*, or kitchen. The Ovvaidon is a large saloon, corresponding in size and position to the Egarathon, and fitted up with equal splendor. The Uvvithon is also a large room in which the viands, intended for the table, are placed previous to being served. The sleeping apartments of the servants are either above or behind these two rooms, for the kitchen is separated from the house by an opening of four or five feet, though under the same roof.

The apartments on the first floor of a two story house are lit by openings in the side walls, near the ceiling, composed of elaborate carving in open work; or else, as in the northern part of the Valley, light is afforded by oblong or oval windows, which are formed of very thin slabs of white jasper, which material varies much from the species of mineral to which it properly appertains, in being transparent, almost as much so as mica. On the second floor, all the rooms are lit by skylights, over which, at noon and at night, awnings are drawn, while in winter, or more properly speaking, during the rainy season, roofs are built, raised about two feet above the opening, so as to admit a little daylight under the eaves, while more finds its way though plates of white jasper set into the temporary roof.

The floors are usually composed either of tesselated marbles, or of marqueterie, composed of woods stained in various colours and arranged in some fanciful or intricate pattern.

The roofs of all buildings are perfectly flat, with parapets of solid masonry, so that were it not for sundry large bronze pipes, in the form of serpents, that ornament the corners of all houses, these roofs would, during the rainy season, be converted into perfect lakes.

The monstrous stone snakes that formed the balusters of the flights of steps in front of '*our*' palace, were hollow, and nothing more nor less than rain pipes on a large scale. How queer they must look with the cascades of water gushing from their capacious mouths.

Gutters are not used, but subterranean pipes are laid from each house to the nearest street, emptying into an enormous stone culvert, extending down the centre of it to the lake of Naloma. The top of this culvert is below the level of the thoroughfare, and I should never have discovered how the system of drainage was carried on, had

I not one day, in my rambles with Grey, stumbled upon a party of workmen repairing a breach, caused by the fall of a large warehouse in the Street of the Factories.

CHAPTER IV.

Domestic Manners and Customs.

In this chapter I shall once more enter the penetralia—the Avvaroga,—of Geralian life, and strive to place before the reader an accurate picture of the way in which the natives employ themselves 'en famille,' and their household arrangements in general.

In the families of the wealthy classes and the nobility, the dignity of the house cannot be properly maintained with less than fifty domestic servants, exclusive of the palanquin bearers, who never number less than sixteen, and the body servants who form the escort of the master of the house when travelling about the Valley in state. Of these fifty, thirty are usually females, and the remainder men and boys, all of whom are under the supervision of the *Milla-il-athl*, or Master of Welcome, a head servant corresponding to the butler of large English establishments. He engages the servants, orders all entertainments, punishes all misconduct, and is a medium between his master and his inferiors in everything except the actual payment of wages.

The female servants are the Avvar-il-Avvaroga, similar to ladies' maids and semstresses, who are always in the apartments of their mistresses, either working with them or attending their toilette. Second, the Avvar-il-Itanalpa, who are under-cooks and scullions beneath the control of the Malla-il-Itanalpa, or chief cook, who also holds her reign over the Avvar-il-Uvvithon (pantry girls) and even over the Ivvar-il-Ovvaidon (male waiters) who form one class of the men servants; a second class is called Ivvar-il-Egarathon (parlour servants) who introduce visitors. A third is termed the Ivvar-il-Evoridua, valets of their master. Then there is the Milla-il-Zilathal, or master of the portico, a sort of porter; and these are found,—except the Ivvar-il-milla (body servants) and Ivvar-il-dalr (palanquin bearers),—in the houses of the rich, their number varying according to the degrees of state affected by their masters. Some are extravagant enough to retain a band of dancing women, a number of musicians, and even have Avvar-il-Ovvaidon, or girls to wait on table as well as men, the former being much more expensive and scarce.

The day of the nobles not attending Inca's court —for then they live in the royal palace, apart from their families,—commences about six o'clock in the morning, when they are awakened by their principal body servant. A bath is then taken at the fountain, after which a slight breakfast is generally partaken of, in private. The nobleman if he has a family, then visits the Avvaroga, and stays there a short time, after which he perhaps goes to his study, if I may so call it, and instructs his sons in such things as it is necessary for them to learn previous to entering the academy of Incas. A visitor may come, or he himself may now order his fomer-dal and proceed to see his friends, returning to dine with his family near dark. It must not be supposed that he fasts eleven hours, for such is not the case, as a lunch is always served at noon, consisting of sweetmeats and pleasant drinks, of which,—if he is at home,—he partakes with his family and such visitors as may chance to be in the house at the time.

The dinner is the leading affair of the day, and consumes over an hour, to do justice to its demands; but as I have previously given a description of a private dinner, sufficiently explicit in its details, this interesting subject can be passed over here. After it is despatched, the evening is passed either at home, at a friend's house, or perhaps at some book store, which are then always thronged with readers. All shopping by gentlemen is done in this portion of the twenty-four hours, by which, of course, we do not mean such buying and selling, as occupies the morning in the Tianguez, and great business streets.

In the dry season, the numerous open squares of the cities, planted with stately trees, and watered by huge fountains, are illuminated during the evening, and are crowded by the lower classes, who have very good refreshments served at a low cost. During the rains, most of these persons remain at home at night; but the rich and the nobility, unite in parties of ten or twelve, meeting at each other's houses on certain evenings, when they discourse upon literary and various matters, read, or in some other simple way amuse themselves.

We now turn to the duties and employments of the female portion of a wealthy Geralian family.

Besides the actual wife of a man, married by ceremony in the Temple of the Sun, or by a magistrate, there are several Odalisques (Ulvamathalr) in every family of wealth, numbering according to the wish and ability of the master from two to a hundred, a limit being there placed by the Inca, who alone is permitted to have more. There are laws which forbid the Ulvamathalr living with their master, unless they receive from him a yearly allowance of a hundred gold ochols, in failure of receiving which, they can summon a magistrate and compel him to pay the money. They live in the same apartments as the mistress of the house, in friendship, work with her, visit, shop or travel in her litters, and in fact, seem like sisters.

The Ulvamathalr are not slaves, as they can leave their master's house, by giving him sufficient notice; but if they attempt to quit it without warning, they are arrested and bound to remain with him until his death, a second effort at evasion being punishable at the master's will. These bond women are called Inlathalr, and might almost be considered slaves, as the power of life and death is vested in their master's hands.

The children of the Ulvamathalr and Inlathalr are educated with those of the mistress of the house, and treated similarly in every way; the same dower is given on their marriage, the same honours at their death. The Inlathalr are not admitted to the society of the Ulvamathalr, except by the express permission of their master, which is frequently given, so that no distinction between the two is recognized, saving in the matter of salary, the former receiving but half as much (fifty gold ochols) as their more honoured companions.

The Geralian race is remarkably noble looking, majestic in deportment, of delicate features and fine form; the complexion is generally a clear and not very dark olive, sometimes so closely approaching what we would call merely a dark skin, that one would almost suppose there was white blood coursing beneath it. The colour is generally rich, if not high; the eyes and hair are black, or very dark brown, the former being large, lustrous, and very expressive; the teeth are invariably like pearls, and the chin and mouth somewhat on the Greek order of beauty. The male portion are seldom under five feet eight inches, and admirably proportioned, while the females are of good height.

We will now speak of the occupations of the mistress of a wealthy citizen's household during the day.

The first rays of the rising sun pierce through the elaborate open tracery of stone which forms the cornice of her chamber, revelling among the deep carvings of the coved ceiling, and playing over the gold embroidered folds of the voluminous hangings, a part of which being swept aside, the malla-il-avaroga enters alone, and approaching the canopied couch of her mistress, awakens her and receives her orders. The Ulvamathalr then enter to pay their morning respects, they having just arisen in the adjoining rooms. The mistress of the house then rises, and attended by the Ulvamathalr and the Avvar-il-Avvaroga, proceeds to bathe at the fountain in the centre of her apartment; or if the morning is oppressively warm, they all go into the surrounding gardens, and make use of one of the numerous artificial lakes that are always constructed in them, enclosed by impervious shrubbery and foliage. After revelling in the cool water for some time, they return to their respective apartments to have their toilettes completed, and about six o'clock reunite in the Ovvaidon-Avvaroga, or women's eating room, where they partake of the first meal of the day. The utensils of gold and silver then used are cleansed and restored to the vast plate chests under the superintendence of the mistress of the house and the Malla-il-Avvaroga.

This done the Ulvamathalr accompany their mistress to the sewing room,—if I may so term it,—where the children of the family join them. The females resume their various occupations of spinning, embroidering, making their dresses, painting,—in which art some are extremely clever,—and writing. While thus engaged they receive the visit of the master of the house, and on his departure with his sons, some of the ladies give instructions on various subjects to the girls of the family, which engrosses the entire morning, until lunch is served at noon. During this time many of the Ulvamathalr have doubtless been out in their palanquins, shopping or visiting, but they are usually home at lunch, subsequent to which they take a siesta, followed by a resumption of their previous employments. About four o'clock, succeeds a bath, followed by a palanquin ride in the surrounding country, or on the mountain terraces, where they sometimes walk,—a visit to the Inca's wife, a saunter in the Street of the Ocelot, or a lounge about the garden until dusk, when the entire family dine together in the great Ovvaidon. In the dry season the evening is frequently spent by the side of the numerous baths in the gardens, or in hamacas swung between the boughs of illuminated trees. Sometimes the ladies accompany the master of the house in his visits to his friends, or perhaps the whole household of a neighbour will come to pass the evening, frolicking in the open moonlit air. During the wet season, large companies of ladies only, are held in the Avvàroga, when they laugh, talk, play with the children, eat, drink, and are perhaps entertained with music, singing, dancing, or some other amusement, the most esteemed being the recitation of poems commemorative of the exploits of former heroic Incas, their bravery in battle, or the romantic history of their amours.

It now remains to note the ceremonies observed in the cases of marriage, birth and death, with which this chapter will close.

Love has but little to do with Geralian marriage:—the father of the youth casts his looks abroad among his friends' daughters, and having found one whose alliance seems advantageous, contrives, with the lady's father, some means by which the future bridegroom shall be introduced to her. After this one interview with the lady, who is probably fourteen, while he is perhaps a year or two older, his father asks him to marry her, which is mere form, for if he refused he would be obliged. Having consented, his father prepares a splendid present for the bride elect, which is sent in the son's name, and a return made in the form of a bouquet of white flowers. All now is arranged, and the two fathers having fixed a day, invite all their friends to meet them at the principal temple of the town in which the parties reside, and preparations are instantly commenced for the ceremonies attendant upon the occasion. On the morning of the eventful day, the bridegroom, attired with great splendour, is conveyed in an open palanquin to the bride's house, attended by his father, mother, and all his relatives and friends. Arrived there, the house is found covered with blue hangings, the doors being concealed by a heavy drapery. The youth alights, and accompanied by two friends, approaches the hidden door: the first friend addresses the unseen inmates of the building, but receives no answer. The second friend does the same with a like result, and the bridegroom advances to the door, which he commands them to open. No attention is paid, and so, drawing a sharp weapon, the youth cuts down the drapery. As it falls numberless servants rush out at a trot, escorting a closed palanquin, in which is the bride and her mother. This draws up at the side of the youth's conveyance, which he has already re-entered. The door of the posei-dal is slid back, and the bride's mother comes forth and stands by it, where she is joined by the father and nearest relations, and by the parents of the bridegroom. The lady is now handed forth to the sound of trumpets, and is placed by the side of her future husband, her features and person completely concealed by an impenetrable veil.

The whole party now proceeds to the great Temple of the Sun, where they are received by the priests and choristers, who escort them to the high altar. The bride and bridegroom are seated before the dais, while a chaunt is sung, and an address made to the Sun by the principal officiator. Offerings are then made to the temple by the parents, and the bridegroom presents a scroll, —and a duplicate of it,—by which the nearest magistrate permits the marriage. Both of these certificates are sanctified by the priest's signature or mark; one is returned to the presenter, and the other is placed in the cabinet, behind the Vase of Sacrifice, after having been fumigated and read aloud. The bride is then borne off to her parent's house, where she remains for three days.

After dark, on the evening of the third day, she is conveyed, veiled as before, to the bridegroom's residence, attended by numerous servants of both sexes, carrying her wardrobe, and lighted torches. Arrived at her destination, she finds the Uthirb-il-athl lit up, and the whole portico thronged with domestics bearing lights. She descends from her palanquin, and is received by the bridegroom's mother. Followed by all the females of the household, she moves toward the Evoridua, where she finds her husband seated alone on the Tarim-ilathl, while soft music is heard proceeding from an unseen band of musicians. She advances to the dais, and pauses at its foot,—the females form a semicircle round her,—the mother comes up behind the bride and unfastening the veil at the crown of her head, it falls to the floor, displaying the lady clad in a splendid *pavisa* of white, richly embroidered in gold. Renewed bursts of music fill the air, and the females all retire to partake of a collation, leaving the young couple together.

Such are the simple ceremonies of marriage; those attending the birth of an infant come next on the list.

These do not commence until the day after the birth. Before sunrise, the Egarathon of the mansion is filled with guests of both sexes. As the very first beams of the sun light the room, the father of the child enters, and the mother is brought in upon a couch. A heavy curtain which has concealed the entrance to the Evoridua, is now swept aside, and all the servants of the family come in, bearing different comestibles, and followed by the Ulvamathalr, the eldest of whom carries a large golden dish on which lies the child covered with a white cloth. All these are clad with the greatest splendor, and move to the sound of music. The father advances, removes the cloth, and taking the child in his hands, carries it round to each of the company, followed by the principal Ulvamathal bearing the golden dish, on which the visitors place all sorts of little trinkets and toys, for the child's use when it shall grow older. The baby is then carried off, and the whole party removes to the Ovvaidon to breakfast.

Three days after this 'Parade of the Child,' it is taken to a temple and named, with comparative privacy, no one being present save the parents and closest connections. In case of the ill health of the infant, the priest comes to the father's house and there performs the ceremony, which consists merely in fumigating the baby over a Vase of Sacrifice, and pronouncing the name,—which the parents wish to bestow upon it,—four times, once to the north, the south, the east, and the west.

There is but little ceremony attending the burial of the dead. As soon as a person dies, the body is surrendered to the embalmists, who, in thirty days, return it to the family. It is then placed upon a high couch or table, and for seventy-two hours is surrounded by the women of the house, who,—in the eastern manner,—beat their breasts, tear their hair, rend their garments and utter horrific yells. This having been performed to the satisfaction of all parties concerned, the embalmed body,—which bears the exact appearance of life,—is placed in an open palanquin, and conveyed by night through the streets, attended by a large torchlight procession, to the walls, without which are the subterranean excavations, appropriated to the reception of the dead. The body is placed in its upright niche, and the escort scampers off as quick as it is able, being afraid to remain anytime in the catacombs.

Ned and I visited one of these excavations toward the end of October, and had much difficulty in obtaining a guide. The entrance was about a hundred yards east of the Coluca Gate, and consisted of a flight of shallow steps leading down some thirty feet below the level of the Lake of Naloma. A turn at the foot of the stairs caused us to face the west, and we saw the immense subterranean halls and corridors excavated from the solid rock, and reaching a full half mile in a straight line. Taking the central hall, we walked the entire distance; throughout it was of equal height and breadth, the former I should say twenty feet, the latter fifty. The walls are filled with niches, six feet high, and two deep, each of which contained an embalmed body, whose name was inscribed on a tablet over the niche, as well as the period of his decease. There must have been ten or fifteen thousand mummies in that hall alone, which was the principal, as on each side of, and running parallel with it, were seventeen other corridors, of slightly smaller dimensions, and the same length, connected by numerous passages, so irregular in form that a person, without a guide, would infallibly be lost. Having reached the end of the great hall, we descended by a staircase, thirty feet lower, where a similar arrangement presented itself; satisfying ourselves with a glance, we ascended to the upper halls and thence to the open air, when we learnt that we had visited one of the smallest excavations about Geral, and yet this hall of the dead must have contained at least 500,000 bodies.

From Valaïon's work, I glean that the immense number of bodies embalmed and placed in these 'rock halls' was caused by the fact of the early high priests of the Sun, having commanded all the dead to be interred in close proximity to the capital city. In order to do this, those who resided at a distance were obliged to embalm their dead to convey them to the designated spot, where they of course were seen by the Geralians. These, struck with the strong resemblance existing between the mummy and the former appearance of the man, gradually adopted embalming, until it has become general. For one hundred and twenty-four years, every one who died in the valley was mummified and en-niched in these excavations around the capital; but it, at length, became inconvenient from the great number of cities, and the vastness of population, so that the Inca Huayna Evora, before mentioned in this book, decreed an excavation to every city in its own environs, in consequence of which, there is absolutely no necessity now for embalmists, but the practice is nevertheless continued. The edict was promulgated in 1655, according to our chronology. Huayna Evora died in 1661.

CHAPTER V.

Pastoral Life.

AFTER so long a chapter on perhaps but an uninteresting subject to most of my readers, they will doubtless be glad to leave the crowded thoroughfares and formal usages of the city, and turn to the ways of life high on the overlooking hills and mountains, or far away on the plains of the valley.

It must be evident to any one who has read the first part of this work, that I personally can know but little of Pastoral Life, as when I passed through the country it was in the escort of the Inca, or in the company of some nobleman of high rank, and I must therefore confess that most of the matter in this chapter is drawn from Valaïon, and, principally, from Dapartesa. I also gathered some information from our good friend Cioaco, the Curaça of Ocopaltepec, who, perhaps is as worthy an authority as either of the above named, from his having spent a great part of his life on his estates, some miles from the capital, mixing with the country people, and knowing much in regard to them.

The rural population of the Valley is estimated to be somewhere in the neighbourhood of 300,000, residing principally in the villages and small hamlets that hang on the terraces of the mountains, or are scattered near the large cities, while but few, comparatively speaking, reside in single houses, for fear of the Lambys and other wild tribes.

The country people are divided into two general classes, farmers, and tenders of llamas. The former cultivate the immense plantations that belong to the state, and transfer the produce to the magazines of the department in which they live. The second class is also divided in two parts, the true llamaherds, who take care of the precious animals, and those who drive them to market, or lead them over the causeways when loaded with merchandise; while both of these classes are subdivided into those employed by the government, and those paid by the manufacturers of woollen cloth.

The females of the families over twelve years of age have a certain portion of spinning to do for the woollen and cotton factories belonging to the government, for which they are paid by the head of the tenth family, (see Chap. I.), who is re-embursed by the state. Under the above age, the children are sent to the district schools, one of which is appropriated to the use of fifty families; and out of each of these institutions five male scholars are annually sent to the capital to enter the College of Amataus, where their education is carried on at the expense of the Inca, while an equal number of girls are also sent to be educated in Geral. When the boys of the rural population attain the age of twelve, a choice of occupation is offered them by the resident inspector; except to the eldest son of every family, who by law follows his father's employment. The younger sons may become as their fathers, may enter the army as private soldiers, learn a trade in the nearesttown, work in the mines or public works, or seek employment as servants in the cities of the Valley: in every case being assisted by the government.

The eldest son, for three years is employed by the various manufactories in snaring birds for the making of the beautiful plumage tapestry, and in other ways rendering himself useful, until his fifteenth birthday, when he is considered by the government in the same light as his father.

The occupation of a farmer on the level of the valley is severe work, from the great heat, but on the terraces it is much cooler, and, in consequence, those who work half the year on the valley, for the other half cultivate the mountain side, and vice versa. This arrangement is conducive to health from the change of air, and to good labour from the effect of this change.

The llamaherds never visit the terraces professionally, except when driving the animals with merchandise, or to market, their dwellings being on the top plateau, and their range between that and the perpetual snow line of the Sierra Paricis. The wages of these people are very good, and added to those which their families receive for spinning, are sufficient to support them very comfortably. An occasional employment, which I am about to describe, is very profitable, from the receipts being entirely their own, and always attainable by manual labour.

To every herd of a thousand llamas seven men are attached, and each thousand has a peculiar mark by which their drivers can recognize their charges in any part of the Valley, and they are so marked in order to render possible the separation of two or more flocks that may have become intermingled. When they feel industrious, or when their finances are at a low ebb, the tenders of a dozen herds meet together, and dividing into two equal portions, one part is left to take care of the united flocks, while each of the remaining half procures a Lalama, (see Chap. II.), with ten or twelve llamas harnessed to it. The whole party, numbering perhaps thirty or forty, then starts, armed with large cutting instruments, for one of the frozen lakes or rain pools high up in the glaciers of the mountains. Having selected a suitable one, they clear it of all new fallen snow, rapidly cut out large blocks, and pack them in the lalamas. As soon as the party has procured all that it can, the llamas are reharnessed to the well loaded vehicles, and the cold regions of the 'hard water,' (the translation of the name they give ice,) are deserted for the nearest city, where the contents of the lalamas are sold at a high price to the nobles, who are glad enough to get it to cool their chocolatl and other drinks. Snow is regularly brought to Geral for the same purpose, as it is easy of access, being almost within the city; but it is not of much use, as it melts too quickly. The principal consumption of it in the Capital, is in packing the ice, it being supposed to prevent the latter from turning into 'soft water,' an effect much to be desired, but not attained in that way.

I cannot remember whether or no, I mentioned in the first part of this work, the fact of wine,—or a description of it,—being manufactured in small quantities for the use of the wealthy. For fear I did not, I will run the risk of repeating the account. There are but two factories in the valley, one in the Atolatepec,—the largest and most prolific,—the other on the southern slope of the Huaxtepec within the walls of Geral. The annual product of both these vineyards does not exceed two hundred gallons, which is divided into three equal portions, one for the Inca, another for such nobles as he may designate, and the third for the High Priest of the Sun, whose agents sell it at immense prices to any one who can afford to buy it. Orteguilla named Ned and I among the recipients of the second third in the distribution, each of us being presented with four bottles, if I may so term earthen jars with narrow necks, holding about three pints. Cioaco sent us two others from his share, thinking we had not received any; we wished to return it, but he obliged us to keep it, and I brought mine home with me, besides three that I had not opened out of the Inca's presents.

It is made of a black grape, and is exceedingly sweet and luscious, so much so that it is absolutely necessary to dilute it with water, in order to render it palatable. When first poured out, it is of a dark red colour, but if allowed to stand, becomes pale pink, while a jar that I opened in July, 1849, was quite yellow, something like sherry, so that I almost thought I had a different sort; the taste, however, was nearly the same, though unquestionably improved by keeping. The vineyards are kept beautifully, on a plan similar to the Italian, growing on horizontal lattice work, and very cool and shady. That on the Huaxtepec was used as a promenade by the Inca and nobles of the highest rank; both are under the direction of an officer, and such care is taken of them, that there is a man for every thirty plants, paid from the Inca's private purse.

Reader :—

I plead guilty to the charge of an unallowably abrupt conclusion, and feel bound to account for this dereliction of duty as well as I may.

While writing these few supplementary chapters, I have become more and more aware of my incapacity to continue, with any accuracy, my accounts of private life, or to make any investigations regarding the working of numerous institutions, whose very titles are unmentioned in the foregoing pages, being known to me scarcely but by name. In my Supplement, I have given as clear an insight, as I am now able, into domestic manners, and am sure, that in carrying out my original plan for this volume, I should fail to do justice either to my subject or to myself.

It is my present intention to revisit, at some close period, the Valley of the Incas, and make a longer stay than I was able to do in 1847, the only drawback being my want of companionship, my good friend Grey being unwilling to leave home for another long absence in a foreign land.

But rather than abandon my project, I would journey alone, in which manner it is more than probable that I shall be obliged to travel.

A. R. MIDDLETOUN PAYNE.

www.ingramcontent.com/pod-product-compliance
Lightning Source LLC
LaVergne TN
LVHW010236110826
845151LV00004B/1308

9781425524579